Doubtful Desire

"Monty, you don't really want to marry me," Davida forced herself to say. "You're just upset by Elspeth's engagement. Why don't you wait awhile. She may well change her mind."

"I don't want her even if she does change her mind, and I don't like a bachelor's existence," Lord Montgomery Pelham declared. He caught Davida up again, and began drawing her, gently but inexorably toward him. "I want my own soft woman in my own bed at night."

Davida's heart was racing as she felt the strangest tremor rush through her. She felt nothing of the fear or discomposure that she had expected. Her head tilted back as Lord Pelham bent ever closer, and she managed only one more attempt at denial. "But Monty, are you saying just any woman will do? Because . . ."

His kiss silenced her tongue . . . it silenced her doubts . . . for this moment of passionate madness, at least . . . until her doubts returned, as sad to say, they surely must, since the man who now held her in his arms still held another woman in his heart. . . .

The Jilting
of
Baron Pelham

by

June Calvin

A SIGNET BOOK

SIGNET
Published by the Penguin Group
Penguin Books USA Inc., 375 Hudson Street,
New York, New York 10014, U.S.A.
Penguin Books Ltd, 27 Wrights Lane,
London W8 5TZ, England
Penguin Books Australia Ltd, Ringwood,
Victoria, Australia
Penguin Books Canada Ltd, 10 Alcorn Avenue,
Toronto, Ontario, Canada M4V 3B2
Penguin Books (N.Z.) Ltd, 182–190 Wairau Road,
Auckland 10, New Zealand

Penguin Books Ltd, Registered Offices:
Harmondsworth, Middlesex, England

First published by Signet,
an imprint of Dutton Signet,
a division of Penguin Books USA Inc.

First Printing, December, 1994
10 9 8 7 6 5 4 3 2 1

This book is dedicated to the members of two local writers' organizations. Central Oklahoma Roundtable of Authors, affectionately known as CORA, focuses on the writing of book-length fiction. OK-RWA, a local chapter of the Romance Writers of America, focuses on the art and business of writing romance fiction.

Thanks to all the members of these two fine organizations—my teachers, my mentors, my friends!

Chapter One

Lord Montgomery Derwent Villars, fourth Baron Pelham, strode along Bond Street, his spirits in strong contrast to the unexpectedly sunny April weather. It had been but two days since the light of his life, Lady Elspeth Howard, had broken their engagement, and Pelham was blue-deviled.

He could not keep himself from thinking of Elspeth. Everywhere he looked his eyes unconsciously sought her guinea gold hair, her lush figure. When a blonde came into view, he immediately compared her to Elspeth, and turned away, disappointed, for who could equal his pocket-Venus with the green eyes?

Suddenly, as if his aching recollection of her charms had conjured her, she appeared not far down the street from him in a spanking red curricle expertly driven by Donald Endicott, Viscount Whitham. She was leaning toward Whitham, dimples showing at either side of her small, perfectly shaped mouth as she laughed at some witticism.

Lord Pelham doubled his fists in anger and turned hastily away. He wouldn't be caught staring at the happy pair. He looked around frantically for a friend to speak to, or a shop to enter, just as Miss Davida Gresham emerged from a mantuamaker directly into his path. She was ladened with packages and laughing back at her similarly burdened maid.

He scarcely knew the young woman, only having met

her once. But far better to be seen conversing with her than staring at his former fiancée like a moonstruck calf.

"Good day to you, Miss Gresham. You look as if you could use some help." Lord Pelham gave her his most charming smile as he began to remove packages from her hands.

Davida Gresham felt her heart give a little kick and then run wild for an instant. She barely knew Lord Pelham, but had admired the handsome nobleman from afar. To find those cobalt blue eyes gazing into hers was startling but thrilling.

A slight sideward flicker of his eyes directed her attention to a flashy curricle just drawing abreast of them. In a second she took in Viscount Whitham's superior smirk and the surprised look on Lady Elspeth's face as she saw Lord Pelham with Davida. The baron's studied lack of awareness of his former fiancée was touchingly obvious. Davida went into action.

"Oh, Lord Pelham," she simpered, drawing near him and smiling her most coquettish smile. "You are too kind and all that is gallant." She laid both hands on his arm and walked down the street, chattering away, leaving her surprised maid sputtering, "But miss, the carriage is this way!"

Pelham was discomposed by this effusiveness, for above all things he hated being toad-eaten. He had not thought the Greshams were bad *ton*, although they were obscure country gentry, known to him only through their friendship with their neighbor, the Duke of Harwood. Just as he was beginning to squirm, wondering how to discourage the familiarity he had so impulsively encouraged a few minutes ago, Miss Gresham looked over her shoulder and then stopped abruptly.

Her eyes were twinkling with merriment. "I think your objective is accomplished, my lord. Lady Elspeth stared at us for as long as she could without tumbling backward out of the curricule. She should be turning quite green by now."

"Green?" Pelham felt vaguely disoriented.

"It *was* your intention to make her jealous by paying attention to someone else, wasn't it? Good strategy, as my father would say, to go on the offensive. Don't let her be the only one to flaunt her beaus."

Davida had begun gently pulling Pelham in the other direction. "My carriage is this way, my lord."

Relief and admiration for Miss Gresham's quick perception flooded Pelham. *So she has been flirting with me to help make Elspeth jealous.* He laughed, beguiled by her sparkling blue eyes, which were filled with flecks of gold.

Something of a connoisseur of female beauty, he quickly approved of her clear fair skin, high coloring, and pert nose. She had a heart-shaped face surrounded by a cloud of short ebony curls barely restrained by a fetching bonnet.

"I thank you for your help, Miss Gresham. As you obviously guessed, I didn't want Lady Elspeth to see me mooning after her like a lovesick hafling."

"Very glad to help, my lord. And after all, it can't hurt my consequences to be squired by Lord Pelham on Bond Street, can it?" There was a gently mocking note to her voice as Davida handed packages in to her maid, who had preceded her into the carriage. Clearly she had not been unaware of Lord Pelham's disdain when he had thought her behavior encroaching.

When she had retrieved all of her packages, Davida reached out a dainty gloved hand and, suddenly serious, said, "I wish you luck, Lord Pelham. I think you want her back."

"Am I so obviously wearing my heart on my sleeve?" Pelham was serious now, too. Somehow he felt he could trust this frank, open-mannered girl.

"You have the right of it, though. I do hope to win her

back. Perhaps you have a good idea. I should try to make her jealous. Lord knows she makes me so." He sighed deeply.

Davida smiled wistfully at him. She wished this handsome auburn-haired young man were sighing for her. She entered her carriage and raised her hand in farewell as he stepped away from the door.

Before she could give John Coachman the office to start, Pelham suddenly jumped back to the side of the carriage. "I say, Miss Gresham, would you help me again? Perhaps you would go driving with me in the park this afternoon? Or tomorrow, if you have plans today?"

Davida had plans, of course, but her parents would declare her mad if she passed up a chance to go driving at the fashionable hour with this top-of-the trees young baron. Their afternoon call on Lady Abernathy would quickly be eliminated from Davida's duties.

"If you will call this afternoon, Lord Pelham, you will save me a very tedious visit with an elderly friend of my grandmama's."

"Excellent!" Pelham thumped the carriage door. "You're a great gun, Miss Gresham! I'll call for you around four-thirty."

Elated, Lord Pelham watched Miss Gresham's carriage pull away. Making Elspeth jealous might be just the thing. As an extremely eligible bachelor, he would normally have to be very careful about paying attention to a marriageable young girl such as Davida Gresham, so as not to give rise to unwarranted expectations. A fellow could even find himself trapped into an unwanted marriage that way! But since Miss Gresham had suggested the idea and shown herself willing to go along with a mild deception, he felt hopeful for the first time since Elspeth had jilted him. She loved him, he was sure. Seeing him paying close attention to another girl was just the thing to bring her to heel.

Jauntily, Pelham turned his steps toward home. He would change clothes and make sure his team and equipment were groomed properly. He wanted to look bang-up to the mark this afternoon.

Davida tripped up the steps of their Brooks Street residence with unladylike haste. Her parents would be in alt to learn of her appointment to drive out with Lord Pelham.

"Peters, where are my parents?" she demanded of their short, stout butler as she dashed through the entryway.

"In the drawing room, miss."

"Tell Cook we will require tea a little early, and some of her best cakes, please." Davida flung herself into the room her mother had redecorated in the fashionable Egyptian motif when they rented the house for the season.

"Mama, Papa, you'll never guess. I'm to go driving with Lord Pelham."

Her father thrust aside his paper instantly, and her mother's hand stayed above the tambour frame, her mouth in a round "oh."

"Papa, it's the most famous thing." Davida quickly narrated her encounter with Lord Pelham for her parents.

"Well, now, well, now," her father murmured, his face flushed with pleasure. "Clever puss. Hooked him, you have. Now you must reel him in."

"No, Papa, you don't understand." Davida knew her father was ambitious for her. The second son of a small landholder, he had been knighted on the field of battle at Saratoga. The death of his older brother had turned him into a reluctant but determined farmer. After successfully courting her mother, the granddaughter of the Earl of Westbury, he had added farm after farm to his original holdings. Now a man of means, he had hopes of a title for his daughter, and perhaps someday a baronetcy or better for his son. And certainly Davida's younger brother, Peter, was a very promising young man, currently distinguishing himself at Harrow. A successful political career might well be possible for him.

Davida frankly thought her father's expectations for her were too high. After several weeks of seeking acceptance among the *haute ton,* she was well aware that titles, with or without fortunes, rarely wed any but those already possessing either one or both. Davida knew herself to be pretty but not a diamond of the first water, and her dowry was merely respectable.

Moreover, she was finding it difficult to gain entrée into the exclusive levels where she might meet the kind of suitors her father wished for her.

Her mother's exalted bloodlines were of little help in introducing Davida to society, as Lady Elizabeth had been the only child of parents who had both died young. The earldom had died out with her grandfather's death, and such connections as Lady Elizabeth had through the Westburys tended to be very elderly people who could offer her daughter little help in the Prince Regent's fast-paced society.

Davida herself would gladly settle for a personable, respectable young man of moderate fortune, but her father was absolutely sure that his darling daughter would marry a lord. He had in fact already run off several promising suitors because they didn't meet his high expectations.

"Understand, Papa, Lord Pelham is not interested in me. He hopes to renew his suit for Lady Elspeth." Not wishing him to be disappointed, nor to misjudge Lord Pelham's intentions, Davida hastened to correct his misapprehension.

"But, Davida," her mother interjected, "he's asked you to go driving."

"After I pointed out that he could make Lady Elspeth jealous by paying attention to me."

"He could have made her jealous with any other female, but you have gained his attention," her father asserted confidently. "He cannot but admire you, once he comes to know you!"

Davida laughed a little nervously. She would do Lord Pelham a great disservice if she raised false expectations in her father. "What I hope is, being seen in his company will help me get noticed. I can assist him with Lady Elspeth, and he can introduce me to his friends. He is well acquainted with the very best people, you know."

"I thought our connection with the Harwoods would have done the trick," her father mumbled.

"Dear Sarah has done her best, but with the duke playing least in sight . . . and while her aunt Helen is very well regarded, she is not very active in the *ton*."

"Yes, yes. I see." Her father frowned. "But you don't want to make an enemy of Lady Elspeth, either. She is on the best of terms with the patronesses of Almack's."

"Oh, Papa." Davida sank into a chaise. "You must give that up. I'll never be invited to Almack's."

"Now, Davida, don't say so. You are as well bred and as pretty as many another girl who goes there every week." Her mother set aside her embroidery to approach her daughter. "And am I not the granddaughter of an earl?"

Her father growled low in his throat. "But I am a mere country squire, Elizabeth. Doubtless I am holding the girl back."

"Never say so, Papa." Davida leaned forward and took her father's hands. "You are a hero and a fine gentleman. The patronesses are terrible snobs. Everyone says so. And if they don't want to know you, I don't want to know them!"

Her father's eyes looked suspiciously moist as he patted her cheeks. "And you are a minx. But a pretty one. That shade of blue suits you."

"I'm so glad you were wearing your prettiest walking dress when you encountered Lord Pelham." Suddenly an alarmed look suffused her mother's countenance. "But you can't wear the same dress for the most important carriage ride of your life!"

Not for the first time since coming to London, Davida felt a sense of panic arising within her. The season might seem like fun and frivolity to many, but to a young girl who must select a husband, these few weeks were of utmost importance, and great seriousness of purpose necessarily underlay her many social activities.

She took herself firmly in hand. She had no wish to disappoint her parents, nor to lock herself into a miserable marriage, so she must keep her wits about her.

"I had thought to wear the yellow carriage dress, Mother."

"We must go upstairs at once and survey your wardrobe." Taking her willing daughter's hand, Lady Elizabeth led the girl from the room as they pondered exactly how Davida should dress for this most significant occasion.

Chapter Two

L ord Pelham arrived promptly and was pleased to find Miss Gresham ready. She drew him to her parents and introduced them. He was pleasantly impressed by Sir Charles's quiet dignity and Lady Elizabeth's poise as they greeted him. There was nothing of the mushroom about any member of this family, he decided with relief.

He graciously accepted a cup of tea and took a small cake from the serving tray, but soon rose. "If you are ready, Miss Gresham, I would like to arrive in the park . . ."

"I know, at the height of the fashionable hour." Davida twinkled at him. "You want positively hundreds of people to tell Lady Elspeth you were seen driving a dashing brunette about."

Lord Pelham laughed. "We understand one another very well." Then, taking a second look he added, "Indeed, you are very dashing in that red spencer."

After much consultation, Davida and her mother had selected a cream-colored muslin carriage dress with scarlet piping, and she wore over it a somewhat daringly colored scarlet spencer with military frogging. It was a fashionable echo of the uniforms of His Majesty's troops. A chip-straw bonnet with scarlet trim framed her face, and she carried a matching cream-and-scarlet parasol.

Davida dimpled up at him as he led her to his curricle.

"Not what every young miss wears, I fear, but I do look so insipid in pastels."

"No one could ever find you insipid, Miss Gresham!" Pelham's gallant response was instantaneous and unaffected. They chatted in perfect harmony as he skillfully maneuvered his curricle and matching bays through the busy London traffic.

As he drove, Davida had the opportunity of studying him. He was such an attractive young man! He had a high forehead onto which tumbled chestnut curls which would be the envy of any girl. In profile his nose was long and straight, and his chin firm. When he glanced at her she noted approvingly the slight cleft to his chin and the high, well-defined cheekbones. His mouth was thin but well shaped and mobile. But the *pièce de résistance* of his appearance were fine eyes so dark blue that they sometimes seemed black, fringed with enviably long dark red-brown lashes.

On this lovely spring day the park was filled with carriages, riders on fine bits of blood and bone, and walkers of every description. Pelham gladly introduced Davida to numerous members of the *ton* who greeted him along the promenade. Davida certainly felt that her objective had been accomplished, for several promising young men seemed most eager to make her acquaintance.

Some of them she had certainly met before, yet being seen with Baron Pelham seemed to give her a certain cachet, just as she had hoped. She was gratified to have several young men ask for the privilege of calling on her.

Lord Pelham did not miss the favorable reaction his companion was receiving. "I'd better make sure you save me two dances at Almack's this evening." He slanted a conspiratorial look at her.

Davida flushed and looked away. "Perhaps at the Stanhope Ball? I do not go to Almack's."

"What nonsense. Why ever not?" Correctly interpreting her silence, he asserted, "I'll speak to Sally myself.

Lady Jersey is an old friend of our family." He threw back his head and laughed with glee. "That will really get back to Elspeth. Lady Jersey and her mother are thick as thieves."

How she loved to see him laugh. Davida admired the strong column of his throat above his cravat, the white gleam of his teeth, the rich, throaty sound he made. The trend of her thoughts surprised her. This would never do. She must remind herself that he was spoken for!

"You love her very much, don't you?"

Pelham's cobalt blue eyes closed for a second in pain. Then he turned a determined look on her. "Yes, and I shall win her back. I know she cares for me, you see. It was a foolish lovers' quarrel."

"I do hope driving out with me will help."

"It can hardly hurt. She isn't speaking to me at all right now." Pelham's mouth drew into a bitter line and he steered the curricle into a less busy path.

"She's such a stubborn, moralistic chit. Tell me, Miss Gresham, would you cut up rough merely because your fiancé went to the pantomime without you, to see Grimaldi perform? Honestly, you'd think *she* were the bishop, not her father!"

Davida smiled. "Perhaps she was jealous that she couldn't go herself. I know I'd love to go. I hear Grimaldi is brilliant."

"Hmmm." Pelham considered this interpretation of his fiancée's behavior, neatly guiding his bays past a knot of pedestrians as he pondered. "It's true that the theater I attended is not such as a gently bred female would wish to be seen at. But no, I doubt that's it. She could go see him at Drury Lane. The fact is, Elspeth has no taste for popular entertainments, and I can accept that. But she disapproves of everything I do except dance attendance upon her. It was just becoming too boring. I don't intend to live under petticoat rule, frankly, and I told her so. That's when she threw my ring at me."

Privately Davida thought their problems seemed deeper than a mere lovers' quarrel, but she felt truly sorry for Lord Pelham. She laid a hand on his arm. "I'm sure she regrets it now. Perhaps you should call on her or send a note and . . ."

"What? Apologize? I'm not sorry. I meant what I said." He set his mouth in a stubborn line.

"Yes, but I daresay you still regret the quarrel. You could say that."

Pelham smiled then, a warm, slightly slantwise smile that made Davida's heart do a sudden flip-flop. "You are a sophist, Miss Gresham."

She laughed. "All's fair, you know."

"Tell, me, Miss Gresham, why haven't I seen you more often this season? You and Lady Sarah Harwood must be two of the most reluctant young ladies to be presented this season."

Her always rosy cheeks took on a deeper hue as Davida denied being reluctant. "It's just that my parents have never made a practice of being in London for the season, and so haven't a wide acquaintance. As for Sarah, the duke is almost reclusive since his wife died five years ago. He simply couldn't face a season in London, so her Aunt Helen, Lady D'Alatri, is bringing her out. She is a very lively and interesting person, but given more to intellectual pursuits than the social whirl."

"Ah, yes, Lady D'Alatri. Something of a bluestocking, is she not? She is very interested in music, I believe. A member of the Philharmonic Society?"

Surprise showed in Davida's voice as she acknowledged this. "Oh, I am not entirely a fribble, Miss Gresham," Pelham assured her, amusement lighting his features. "I play several instruments, and though I cannot hope to attain the proficiency that would gain me entry into the Philharmonic Society, I never miss one of their concerts if I can help it."

"What instruments do you play, Lord Pelham?"

Davida was captivated that this handsome young man, who inclined toward the Corinthian, should be so musical.

"Well, I play the piano rather well, the violin somewhat better, and the flute very badly. This winter I believe I will take up the cello. If someone in our county can learn it, we would have a fairly good string quartet. Are you musical, Miss Gresham?"

Davida was pleased to be able to answer in the affirmative. "I suppose you could say my instrument is my voice, though I can play the piano respectably. My greatest delight so far in London has been to hear the operas presented at King's Theatre."

With a quirk to his mouth that said he knew the answer already, he asked, "Why do you specify King's Theatre?"

Davida was entirely serious in her reply. "Oh, at Covent Garden and Drury Lane they quite butcher them, making tragedies end happily, interrupting scenes of great intensity for some burlesque. It is just too bad of them. They simply ruined a production of Mozart's *Don Giovanni* that I particularly wanted to hear performed as it was written."

"You sound almost fierce, Miss Gresham."

Embarrassed, Davida turned away. "I should be more careful. A young lady shouldn't take anything seriously but her gowns and her bonnets, I'm told."

He laughed again, that marvelous deep laugh, and reached out a hand to turn her face to his. "That sort of young lady is a dead bore, Miss Gresham. And I entirely share your opinions. I take my opera very seriously; in fact, I sometimes attend final rehearsals, in order to hear the music without the obnoxious noise the audience makes during performances."

"Do you really? How I wish I could do that!"

"I don't know if that would be possible." He hesitated

a minute. "You see, sometimes the musicians and directors are rather rough-spoken when mistakes are made."

"Oh." Davida lowered her head in disappointment. "Mama would never let me go then. She is most strict."

Pelham looked at the crestfallen girl sympathetically. "I understand. I have a very strict mother, too. And my father, when he was alive, was an absolute paragon of propriety." An awkward silence drove him to change the topic.

"You and Lady Sarah are very good friends, I believe."

"Oh, yes, almost like sisters. We were practically raised together. We are related, you know. Double third cousins or some such thing."

Pelham looked intrigued, but before he could pursue the topic further, they were hailed by a friend of Davida's, Lieutenant Reginald Prescott of the Royal Guard.

Davida's cheeks pinked when she saw who it was. She very much suspected that Lieutenant Prescott had offered for her and been turned away by her father. From his friendly manner, he apparently bore her no ill will, however.

"Give my regards to your father, Miss Gresham," he urged her as he turned his horse to trot alongside them. "Regular Tartar, Sir Charles. Look out for him, my lord. He was my father's commanding officer in the colonial war."

Pelham grinned and turned to her. "I didn't realize your father was a military man, Miss Gresham."

Proudly Davida informed him that her father had served with distinction, advancing to Lieutenant colonel and receiving a knighthood as a result of his service. "He was with General Cornwallis when he surrendered. The general hinted he might receive a title but it never came to pass."

Pelham wryly observed, "Losing a war, especially an

unpopular one, is not, I suppose, the best route to advancement!"

Davida laughed. "I suppose not."

"Wish I'd gotten my colors before we licked Boney," Lieutenant Prescott asserted. "What I wouldn't give to see some real fighting."

As they parted from Prescott, Pelham observed, "He might not be so sorry it was over if he had any true sense of his own mortality. My younger brother was just like him. If he were still here, I wouldn't be in quite such a push to marry."

"What . . . what happened, if you don't mind telling me?"

"No, I'm very proud of Theodore. Like your father, he was a war hero. My father didn't want him to fight, being ardently opposed to the restoration of the Bourbon dynasty, but Theo was hot-blooded, and very impatient with being a younger son. So father bought him his colors. He was killed during the storming of Montmartre in 1814."

Pelham stopped and looked away for a moment, obviously composing himself. "Only twenty—so young to die! But before he died he was much decorated and praised in the dispatches. Father was proud of him, no matter how he felt about the cause."

Davida nodded. "Yes, I can understand that he would be." Remembering her younger brother Peter's intense interest in all things military, she glanced curiously at Pelham. "And you, did you never wish to follow the drum?"

"At one time it had its attraction, but I am, like my father, too much the Whig to wish to go to arms to restore the Bourbons. At any rate, as the oldest son and heir, I was made firmly aware of my duty to remain at home, to safeguard the name and learn how to manage our estates."

"Well, at least now I know how to deflect my father's

aspirations." Davida spoke without thinking, then blushed deeply when Pelham insisted on an explanation.

"You see, my father is quite determined I shall marry a title or a fortune, or both."

"What father isn't?" Pelham teased.

"I am glad you can joke about it! I find this mercenary approach to matrimony very disagreeable. It must be tiresome for you to always be fending off matchmaking parents. At any rate, if Papa begins to hear wedding bells when you call on me, I'll just tell him you're a confirmed Bonopartist. That will put him off."

Pelham grinned appreciatively. "He's a strong Tory, then?"

"The staunchest. God, King, and Country! He has no patience with any but the strictest loyalist views."

"We are not so far apart as you think, Miss Gresham. I am all for God and Country, and the King, too, as long as Parliament can keep him on a short chain." He winked wickedly at her and whipped up his team.

Their ride ended as pleasantly as it began, and Lord Pelham secured the promise of two dances at the Stanhope ball the following Saturday, but archly warned her he still intended to collect two at Almack's soon, as well.

Davida watched the tall, elegant form stride away, firmly suppressing a strong twinge of regret that he wasn't interested in her. She hastened up the stairs, eager to tell her parents of her success in the park. There were several very eligible young men planning to call on her, and wouldn't her father be in alt to hear that Lord Pelham thought he could obtain vouchers for Almack's?

Chapter Three

The next morning Davida's best friend, Sarah, daughter of the Duke of Harwood, called on her, full of excitement. "Oh, Davie," she breathed as she rushed into the morning room where Davida was alone, lingering over breakfast and the newspapers. "You'll never guess what was all the talk at Almack's last night!"

Davida smiled affectionately at her plump blond friend. It had been hoped by both girls that Sarah's father's sponsorship would have been enough to secure invitations to Almack's for Davida, but as yet it hadn't happened. Still, Sarah had faithfully introduced her to those members of the *ton* with whom she was acquainted, and the two had gone together whenever they both had invitations to the same event.

"Such a dust-up! You cannot credit it! Good morning, Cousin Elizabeth."

Davida's mother came into the room looking rather distracted. "Good morning, Sarah. Davida, dear, have you seen my half-glasses?"

"I believe you left them on the piano, Mother."

"Come listen, Cousin Elizabeth. You'll be amazed at the latest *on-dit*!" Sarah gave an enthusiastic little bounce as she motioned Lady Elizabeth to a chair.

"By all means." Davida's mother settled herself, all eagerness.

"Well, you know that Lady Elspeth Howard jilted

Lord Pelham?'' Mother and daughter exchanged interested glances and nodded their heads.

"Last night he asked her to stand up with him, and she
said, right out loud so everyone could hear, 'I don't
dance with men who flaunt their fancy pieces in the park
for all to see'!'"

Davida and Lady Elizabeth drew in identical breaths
of dismay. Sarah, unaware of any undercurrents, hurried
on. "And Lord Pelham got very cold and icy and said
that the girl he was driving with was all that was respectable. And then Lady Elspeth said, 'Strange, I do not
see her here tonight.' "

"Oh, dear," Lady Elizabeth moaned.

"Wait, you haven't heard the whole. Lord Pelham's
face turned brick red, and he fairly snarled at her, 'But
you shall see her when I escort her to the Stanhope ball
Saturday.' "

Then she said, in the most cutting tone, "And shall she
be wearing scarlet and pantaloons again?" Whereupon
he not only walked away from her, but left Almack's."

Sarah waited for some comment or question from her
two auditors, but it was slow in coming, so she added, "I
can't wait until Saturday to see who it is, can you?"

"No, no indeed," Davida managed. "Did no one know
her?"

"Well, as to that, there was all sorts of speculation,
everything from Lord Pelham's truly planning to bring a
fancy piece to the ball, to its perhaps being Lady Mercer.
But I've saved the best, and funniest, for last. Guess
what it is?"

Davida shook her head. "I can't." But she had a strong
feeling that she could.

"Sir Charles Moresby said it was you. Told me, 'You
know the gel, I daresay. Miss Gresham is a bosom bow
of yours, ain't she? And Lord Threlbourne thought it
was you, too. Said Lord Pelham had introduced you to
him in the park."

"What did you say?"

"Oh, of course I said it couldn't have been you, you scarcely know Lord Pelham."

Davida chuckled ruefully. "Knowing him is turning out to be more dangerous than I thought."

For the first time the look of glee faded from Sarah's round face. "What do you mean, Davie?"

"I mean, it was I who was driving with Lord Pelham in the park yesterday."

"Never say so, Davie!"

"I am afraid it's true. I was wearing my scarlet spencer. You know the one." Then Davida told the whole story to Sarah, who clapped her hands and pronounced it famous. "And it certainly worked, for Lady Elspeth was furious."

"It worked, but did it help or hurt?" Davida's brow knit in a worried frown. "It sounds to me like it drove them even further apart. I hope he does not repent it."

"And I hope you do not repent the day ever you laid eyes on Lord Pelham," her mother moaned. "I should have vetoed the pantaloons. No matter how lacy and decorative they are, some *will* persist in seeing them as fast."

"Princess Charlotte wears them," Sarah defended her friend staunchly.

"And on a breezy day in the park, I think them much more apt than petticoats to preserve the decencies," Davida insisted.

At that moment, Perry carried in a card on a tray and handed it to Lady Elizabeth. Noting the turned-down corner, she read it, her brows lifted in surprise. "Yes, of course, Perry, show him in."

She smiled archly at the two curious girls, obviously enjoying their puzzlement until moments later Lord Pelham swept into the room.

Davida felt a tightening of her breath as he drew near. Really, the man was too attractive, and especially now, for this morning he wore an air of serious purpose, rather than the boyish vulnerability she had seen yesterday.

"Lady Elizabeth, Lady Sarah, Miss Gresham." He greeted each one and seated himself across from Davida.

Davida felt a curious little flutter to her heart's rhythm as she looked at Pelham, so handsomely attired in a form-fitting brown morning coat. His neck stock was rather casually tied, and he wore the fashionable trousers.

"Lady Sarah has perhaps told you something of what happened at Almack's last night?"

"Yes, it seems I am become a fancy piece. I should have known better than to wear that scarlet spencer." Davida smiled archly at him.

Pelham frowned. " 'Tis no laughing matter, I fear. Her careless words have unleashed a storm of speculation. Betting at White's, scandal broth likely being served with tea this morning. You know how the *ton* loves a scandal. The last thing I wanted to do was to risk your reputation."

"And the last thing I wanted to do was to make things worse between you and Lady Elspeth."

Sadness softened Pelham's features for an instant, but then he returned to his purposeful mien. "I wish to request the opportunity to escort you to the Stanhope ball. My mother will be accompanying us."

"Bringing up the siege guns, Lord Pelham," Lady Elizabeth observed.

Pelham smiled grimly. "We shall need the best weapons at our command."

Davida shook her head. "I thank you, Lord Pelham, but I have long since planned to attend with Lady Sarah and her aunt."

Pelham half bowed in his chair toward Sarah. "I shall be glad to escort you and your aunt, too, Lady Sarah. To continue Lady Elizabeth's metaphor, we can use all the reinforcements we can get in this battle."

Sarah responded as Davida knew that she would. "Of course. My aunt will be delighted to renew her acquaintance with your mother. She often speaks with pleasure of their come-out together."

"But your mother is not well," Lady Elizabeth remonstrated. "Did I not hear that she is an invalid?"

"She suffers from rheumatism and goes about very little, but she agrees with me that this step is entirely necessary, else Elspeth's hateful remark could lead to Davida's social ruin."

Davida sat back, stunned. "It is very serious, then."

"Very."

"Yes, I thought so when Sarah told the tale." Davida's mother nodded her head. "We deeply appreciate your standing by her in this."

"It is only right that I do so. In fact, I hope to take Miss Gresham with me now to meet my mother. She wishes to know her before introducing her to Lady Jersey." He bent his gaze on Davida, determination flashing in the dark, intent eyes.

Davida rose, giving him her hand. "Thank you, my lord. I will be pleased to come with you."

"Don't look so solemn, Miss Gresham. Remember, whatever happens at the Stanhope ball, you will have the pleasure of my company to look forward to." A roguish twinkle lit his eyes.

She laughed. "Oh, indeed, sir. For that I will endure any scandal."

"And rightly so!" Lord Pelham chuckled softly.

"Davida will need to change clothes if she is to accompany you now," Lady Elizabeth observed. Davida was dressed in a simple round gown of yellow sprigged muslin, and had on a frilly cap. And pantaloons! Her mother dropped her eyes significantly, and Davida nodded that she had understood the message.

"Wear that charming blue dress you had on the other morning when you rescued me from making a cake of myself in front of Lady Elspeth."

Davida nodded, flattered that he had noticed her favorite dress, and hurried upstairs. After her maid had swiftly helped her remove the offending pantaloons and change into the blue walking dress, Davida took a moment to tidy her hair. The visage that looked back at her from her mirror was unfamiliar. Instead of her usual naturally rosy countenance, she beheld a pale, frightened face.

With a shaking hand Davida replaced her brush and pinched her cheeks to give them some color, before donning the leghorn bonnet she had purchased the day before. How long ago that seemed! Just this morning she had arisen feeling smugly excited that she had begun to make progress in the *ton*. Now, because of her impulse to assist Lord Pelham, she was on the brink of complete social ruin.

Lord Pelham's mother was a pleasant, friendly person who seemed very disposed to like Davida. Rheumatism had left her somewhat bent and with gnarled hands, but Lady Pelham was still an attractive woman, whose graying red hair suggested the source of the red glints in her son's deep brown curls.

She received them in a charming drawing room which had been cleverly decorated to include some fine older pieces of furniture along with the more modern, lighter furniture. Though all was understated, with no ostentatious display, Davida had no doubt that everything in the room was of the first quality, and some of the paintings were doubtless priceless.

Lady Pelham quickly put the somewhat overawed Davida at ease by a low, chuckling laugh very like her son's as she ventured, "You may perhaps be beginning to regret attempting to help my son get his ox from the ditch since it seems to have landed your own there straightaway."

"I greatly fear it is a case of fools rushing in, Lady Pelham."

"No, the foolish one is our naughty Lady Elspeth. She has a rash tongue when she is upset, I fear." Lady Pelham's soft, cultured voice subtly conveyed her disapproval.

"I do not know her well, but she is very lovely," Davida murmured.

"True. And blondes are all the rage now. At first I feared Monty was attracted merely by her beauty. Her features are quite classical. And it was something of a triumph to catch the acknowledged toast of the season, wasn't it, my dear?" She shot a shrewd glance at her son, who frowned uncomfortably at his parent. "She has many other fine qualities, however. If she can learn to moderate her behavior she will make my son a good wife. He tells me you are related to the Duke of Harwood."

Startled by the change in topic, Davida stammered, "Yes, because in a manner of speaking, my father and he each provided the other with brides."

"Oh, good. I sense a romantic tale!" Lady Pelham settled back against the cushions, smiling encouragingly at Davida. "Do go on, dear."

"My father should be the one to tell it, I suppose. He delights in recounting how His Grace used to run tame in our home as a young man. You see, though Sarah and I are of an age, my father is twenty years older than His Grace. The old duke was a rather cold, forbidding man, Papa says, with little time for his sons."

"Ah, yes, but as I recall, Lord Stephen had plenty of time for gaming!" Lady Pelham grimly summed up the previous duke.

"Yes, I believe so. At any rate, after father came back from America . . ."

"He served in the colonies, then?"

"Oh, yes!" Davida's pride was evident in her voice and radiant expression. "As I explained to Lord Pelham yesterday, my father was knighted there. But when his older brother died, he had to sell out and come home, as my grandmama was all alone, with no one to run the estate. So Papa began to learn all about agricultural improvements. He had never planned to be a farmer, but he's a very proud man, and whatever he does, he wishes to do well at it."

"An admirable trait," Lord Pelham interjected. He gave Davida an encouraging smile.

"His Grace—I mean Viscount Barton, as he then was—admired it, I suppose, for from the time when he was about seventeen, as I heard the tale, he and his younger brother practically lived with my father. He wanted to learn all there was to know about farming, for he intended to improve his land instead of wasting his life on gaming as his father was doing."

A restless movement on Lady Pelham's part warned Davida she had better get on with her tale. "My father was somewhat famous in our county when he returned from the war, so one day the old duke invited him to the abbey to meet his guests. Among them was his cousin, the Earl of Westbury, and his granddaughter, my mother."

A quirked eyebrow told Davida that Pelham had not realized she was so well connected. Satisfied with the effect, she continued. "My mother was quite impressed with my father. Even today, she loves to reminisce about how handsome he was in his military regalia. But she was very shy. She couldn't bring herself to speak to him. So His Grace—I mean Viscount Barton—took matters in his own hands. He told my father he should make a push to get to know the tall, shy girl in the corner, because she had a fancy for him, and a fine dowry, too, with no restrictions on it."

Pelham's laugh rang out. "An irresistible combination for your father, I gather."

Davida frowned. She had not meant to depict her father as a fortune hunter. "My father loves my mother very much. And he used her dowry wisely, to the benefit of herself and her children. He has become the second landowner in the county, after the duke."

"I'm sure Monty meant no criticism, Miss Gresham." Lady Pelham leaned forward to pat Davida's hands while smiling indulgently at her son. " 'Tis very much the way of the world. But I admire your loyalty to your father. So that is how the duke gave your father his bride. And did I understand you to say he returned the favor?"

Davida nodded. "A year later he accompanied my father to visit a relative who had some exotic sheep for sale. There His Grace met my father's second cousin and fell in love with her. Though he was only eighteen, he determined to marry her or no one."

"So young! And pray tell, how did Lord Stephen take that?"

"He took it very badly, as you can imagine, and not just because of his son's age. Cousin Eleanor, like my father, was the offspring of a mere country squire, far below the notice of the heir to a dukedom. The match was forbidden. The duke introduced his son to many eligible females, and even tried to arrange a marriage, but without success."

"For three years they waited for one another. On the day of his majority Viscount Barton had the banns cried in our parish church, and they were wed three weeks later."

"Did his father come to accept her?" Pelham's curiosity was obviously as great as his mother's.

"Not for some time. He refused to even meet her until . . ." Davida's cheeks pinked and she stumbled a bit. "That is . . . when she began increasing. The old duke was dying, and most eager for his son to have an heir, so he relented. He died before Sarah was born, however."

"I suppose in a way that's to the good." At Davida's questioning look, Pelham explained, "If he had not died, he would have been most disappointed in a daughter, I expect. And I believe Sarah is the only child?"

"Oh, I see what you mean. Yes, he would have been devastated if there had been no heir. But there is a younger brother, remember. By now he has three sons, so Harwood has no concerns about the succession."

"That is a charming story, my dear, and it certainly sets my mind at ease about introducing you to Sally Jersey. The granddaughter of an earl and a near connection of a duke, with a war hero for a father, certainly need not fear to apply for vouchers for Almack's." Lady Pelham rang for tea, and asked Davida to pour.

Although it was quite unexceptional for Pelham's mother to ask a guest to pour when her own hands were so crippled, Davida was aware by the keen way Lady Pelham watched her that she was still on trial. However, after she acquitted herself gracefully at this task, the dowager seemed much satisfied. As she was rising to leave, Lady Pelham assured her, "I will ask Lady Jersey to call on me, and introduce you at the Stanhope ball. She will be quick to see your merit."

Tears stood in Davida's eyes at the kindness she saw expressed in Lady Pelham's face. "Thank you, ma'am. I shall do my very best to deserve your patronage."

"A very prettily behaved child, Monty. In future you must be more careful how you involve others in your lovers' quarrels!" After this stern admonition, Lady Pelham waved them away with a smile.

When Lord Pelham had returned her to her anxiously waiting parents, Davida was pleased to be able to give them a favorable report. She had won over Lady Pelham. But still to be answered was whether that grande dame could win over the rest of the *ton*.

Davida's father was quite perturbed when he learned that his daughter was in danger of being considered Lord Pelham's fancy piece. He almost forbade her to have anything more to do with her new friend. Her mother had to exert herself considerably to talk him around.

With a good deal of trepidation Davida prepared herself as best she could for the Stanhope ball, where she might be received into the very highest levels of society—or where she might receive the cut direct from everyone!

Chapter Four

Davida was promised to Lady D'Alatri that Thursday evening, to attend a lecture on mesmerism. When she returned, Perry informed her that her parents wished to see her in the library.

The library was her father's sanctuary, away from the crocodile couches and sphinx chairs he disdained; to be summoned there was sufficiently unusual to make Davida uneasy.

"Yes, Papa?" she queried, nervously fingering a stray curl.

Sir Charles grinned at her. "Don't look so alarmed, child. You're not here for a scold. Your mother and I have been holding something of a council of war."

"War, Papa?" She returned his smile and slid into the indicated chair. Her parents were sitting side by side on a leather sofa, and she had the strong feeling that just before she'd entered the room they'd been sitting much closer to one another.

"Yes, Davie, war! Petticoat doings, to be sure, but no less serious for all that. Now, about the gown you've chosen for the Stanhope ball. Your mother tells me you initially had some doubts about its modesty, but that fancy French modiste talked you around. Is that true?"

A blush spread over Davida's cheeks. The gown was of a deep rose color which she favored because it was highly flattering to her coloring. But the bodice had alarmed her by its plunging neckline, especially when the modiste had virtually ordered her to wear one of the new "divorce" corsets to lift and separate her bosom.

"You have zee nice leetle figure, ma'amzelle, *mais certainment* not what will demand the *gentilhomme's* attention, *non*? But with my design, you will be the cynosure of all eyes."

To her mother's demur she had responded forcefully, "*C'est le dernier cri*, I assure you, *madame*."

"Your mother has confessed to me that she had doubts about that gown, and I see by those flags in your cheeks that you still do."

"Yes, Papa."

"We cannot risk anything daring now, Davie," her mother explained. "I confess it was wrong in me to let Madam talk us into it. I think you should wear another gown instead. It is doubtless too late to have another one made, so we will have to select something very demure from your wardrobe."

A happy thought occurred to Davida. "There's the one that she has yet to complete. You know, the pale green lawn."

"Yes, I had quite forgotten it. It is unexceptionable. We'll call on her tomorrow and make sure it will be ready by Saturday."

"Well, that's settled then. Now that you have your uniform, my little soldier, what do you say to some reinforcements?"

Davida crossed the room and knelt in front of her father. "Oh, Papa, you're thinking of going with us!" Her father detested balls and routs, and routinely avoided them if at all possible.

Sir Charles ruffled his daughter's dusky curls. "If you don't think I'll spoil your campaign?"

She took his hand and held it to her cheek. "I'd like to have you there above all things."

His voice was husky as he raised her. "Then your mother and I will take our carriage, as Lord Pelham's will be quite full. Now run along to bed and get some rest. A well-rested soldier fights best!"

Davida hugged both parents fervently and dashed up the steps, tears in her eyes. Her prayers that night were that she not let her parents down, but somehow be a credit to them.

The Stanhope ball was, in some ways, anticlimactic after all the nervous excitement leading up to it.

Davida had urged her seamstress to finish the new gown of pale mint green lawn, with a demure smocked bodice, high waist, and tiny puffed sleeves. The hem was caught up in scallops to reveal a lacy white underskirt. Worn with the pearls her father had given her for her eighteenth birthday, it was all that was proper for a young lady in her first season.

Madame Poincarré had designed it for her rather disdainfully, as suitable for evenings with elderly maiden aunts and the like. Now it loomed as the single most important gown in Davida's wardrobe!

She spent an unusual amount of time on her toilet that night, nearly driving her maid frantic with requests to try her hair, first one way, and then another, before settling on her usual simple style of curls brought forward around her face, anchored with a ribbon that matched her gown. A matching plume was artfully pinned to the ribbon to curl enticingly along her left ear.

Davida, Sarah, and Sarah's aunt, Lady D'Alatri, were accompanied by Lord Pelham and his mother, as planned. Even as agitated as she was, Davida could not help noticing and sighing over the handsome figure her escort cut in his evening clothes. He looked wonderful in black, and the form-fitting evening britches and knit hosiery emphasized his muscular, well-shaped legs. Once again Davida must needs firmly remind herself that Lord Pelham was not free.

His friendly manner and his mother's graciousness did

much to put her at ease on this night of trial by *ton*. Still, her heart raced frantically as they began the ascent of the stairs leading to the Stanhope ballroom. So *much* depended on this!

She looked behind her and gathered courage from her father's encouraging wink.

The Stanhopes greeted Lady Pelham most courteously and gave Davida a warm welcome as she followed. She was dimly aware of their cordial greetings to the rest of the party as she moved into the crowded ballroom to meet her fate.

"Stay close to me awhile, child," Lady Pelham admonished Davida. "I wish to introduce you to Sally Jersey and several other of my friends."

As Davida was introduced about, flanked by Pelham on one side and his mother on the other, it quickly became apparent that the *ton* had made up its collective mind that here was no fancy piece, but a very respectable young lady. Her dance card began to fill, and her father was gratified by the number of titles represented on that tiny scrap of paper.

Lady Elspeth and her mother, Lady Howard, had already arrived when the Pelham party made their entrance. Davida had been aware, from Pelham's manner, that he knew exactly where they were, as did she. At last their party made its leisurely, apparently random, way to the Howards.

"I wish **you** to know Miss Davida Gresham," Lady Pelham informed them in a commanding tone.

Lady Howard inclined her head graciously. "May I present my daughter, Lady Elspeth Howard." She laid her hand on Elspeth's arm, calling that blond beauty's attention from the small court of admirers standing in a half circle around her.

Davida braced herself for hostility, but either Lady Elspeth felt none, or had herself too well in hand to show it, for she greeted Davida cordially, acknowledging that they had met briefly before. "Was it not at the Wilber-force's musicale?"

Davida nodded. "Yes, where you sang so charmingly that difficult aria from *Orfeo ed Euridice*."

"I feel that we neglect Gluck too much now, in favor of the newer composers, don't you?" Lady Elspeth beamed at Davida as she nodded in agreement. Her pleasure seemed genuine at the compliment, and she turned with perfect ease to Pelham, who was standing stiffly by Davida's side.

"Oh, do stop looking so grim, Monty!" She tapped him on the arm with her fan. "I'm sorry that I spoke so rashly the other night. Your friend is indeed all that is respectable, and excessively pretty besides." She smiled at Davida and pulled her over to introduce her to the young men standing nearby.

While they clamored for a dance, Davida noticed from the corner of her eye that Lord Pelham was writing his name on Elspeth's dance card. She suppressed a brief twinge of pain and told herself stoutly that she was glad to see the reconciliation.

Sometime later she stood with her mother near Lady Pelham's chair. Her father had long since taken himself off to the card room. They watched Pelham and Elspeth dance a waltz as if they had practiced for hours. Davida declined all offers to waltz, not wishing to give any cause for rejection by the autocratic patronesses of Almack's.

Though Lady Pelham's rheumatism must have been causing her pain, she smiled mistily as she watched the waltzing couple. She lifted a crippled hand to grasp Davida's. "Many thanks, my dear. It looks as if your notion of making Elspeth jealous has worked. How good to see them together again, where they belong."

"If I was of assistance, I am extremely glad, my lady. It is clear that he adores her."

"Yes, and she is so good for him. Such a moral and

dutiful girl. She'll cure him of his wild starts and settle him into an excellent husband."

Davida couldn't help feeling that it would be a pity to tame Lord Pelham too much. He wasn't so very wild, after all, and she liked that little touch of the rogue about him.

Just then Sarah's aunt, Lady D'Alatri, strolled up, leading none other than Lady Jersey, who also commented with pleasure on seeing Lord Pelham and Lady Elspeth together again. Lady Pelham made the introductions, and after a few moments of desultory small talk, Lady Jersey turned her full attention on Davida and her mother. "I would like to call upon you next week, if I might?"

Heart pounding, Davida heard her mother assure the patroness that they would be at home on Tuesday afternoon. As Lady Jersey left, Lady Pelham looked up at Davida and winked. "You'll soon have vouchers for Almack's, my dear. Not a bad night's work at all, hmmm?"

Lady Jersey called on Tuesday afternoon as promised, bringing with her Mrs. Drummond Burrell. When Davida, nervously chatting with two young men with whom she had danced at the Stanhope ball, heard Mrs. Burrell announced, she nearly fainted. As if it was not enough to have the talkative, seemingly affable but often unkind Lady Jersey. Oh, no! She also had to pass inspection by the haughtiest, most top-lofty of the patronesses, Mrs. Burrell.

To her surprise, her mother brightened when this exalted personage was announced. All became clear when, after the usual stiff courtesies, Lady Elizabeth reminded Mrs. Burrell that the Westburys were related to the Duke of Ancaster, who was Mr. Burrell's uncle.

The two patronesses and Lady Elizabeth quickly became involved in a convoluted genealogical discussion from which Davida was largely excluded. Finally Mrs.

Burrell turned to her just-discovered connection's daughter. "Now I think of it, you have something of the look of the Ancasters," she informed Davida.

Davida was suitably thrilled to be informed that her heart-shaped face had such a distinguished lineage.

"But the Ancasters always have a widow's peak," Mrs. Burrell intoned dismissively.

"Amazing. We have often wondered from whence Davida got hers. Dear, push the curls off your forehead and let Mrs. Burrell see."

Davida suppressed a surprised laugh. Her parents had often told her that her heart-shaped face and pronounced widow's peak were an inheritance from her paternal grandmother. Now her mother was attributing it to the very distant maternal relationship with the Burrells!

Dutifully Davida exposed her widow's peak for the patroness's interested evaluation. "Just as I said, blood will tell," the grande dame announced pugnaciously. "You should style your hair to show off that distinguished feature, young lady."

Davida assured the patroness that she would do just that.

The three older women, now bosom beaus, began to discuss Princess Charlotte's interesting condition, while Davida turned back to converse with her young gentlemen callers.

When their distinguished guests had left, and the last gangly, eager suitor had inhaled the last piece of lemon cake, kissed her hand, and departed, Davida looked anxiously to her mother.

Whether they had succeeded or failed with the patronesses of Almack's, Davida could not guess, but her mother was supremely confident. "We'll have the vouchers in time to attend tomorrow, mark my words!"

Davida's father was regretful at what he regarded as Davida's folly in "tossing back" Lord Pelham. But when the coveted vouchers for Almack's arrived as her mother had predicted, sent by special messenger Tuesday evening, he grunted in satisfaction. He was equally pleased that many of her partners at the Stanhope ball had not only paid duty calls on her, but sent her flowers, and she was besieged with invitations to go driving or attend various events.

"Any of those young bucks catch your fancy, Davida?" He looked hopefully at her across the dinner table as they discussed her increasingly full social calendar.

"I don't know any of them well, yet, Papa." That sense of panic that Davida often felt rose up, closing her throat.

"The season is passing swiftly, m'dear."

Davida crumbled a croissant restlessly. "Yes, Papa, I know. But two or three months is not long to choose something so important as a husband. You would not wish me to err by acting in haste?"

"No, but I would not wish you to dally, either. This season business costs the earth, and your mother and I detest all these balls and folderol. I hope to see you safely riveted so I don't have to endure a second season."

"Charles." There was a warning note to her mother's voice.

Anxious to avoid a confrontation, Davida essayed a mischievous grin. "Why did you not just sell me to old Lord Tarkington, then?" That ancient roué had astonished them all by offering for Davida at the first of the season. At the time her father had swiftly declined; he wanted a title for his daughter, but not at such a price.

"The nerve of that old, disease-ridden rake," he had exploded, half apoplectic at the thought of giving his beloved daughter to such a creature, titled or not.

But tonight he chuckled and reached across to tousle Davida's short black curls. "Don't tempt me, you cheeky little baggage," he growled.

Davida was surprised and pleased when Lord Pelham called the next afternoon. "I understand you have your vouchers for Almack's," he began, a rather impish look on his face.

"Indeed I do, my lord, I thank you. And do you have your *belle idéal* safely in your pocket again?"

"No, because she persists in trying to put *me* in hers! I think she needs another dose of medicine."

"I hope you don't intend *me* as physic, sir!" Davida had decided she did not relish the false role she had been playing. It was dangerous for her, as the near disaster they had just weathered clearly showed. And it might be dangerous for Lord Pelham as well, for he could have been worse off than before with Lady Elspeth. And she could not like her father's continued notion that Pelham should be considered a suitor. But Pelham evidently didn't share her doubts.

"In a manner of speaking. I would like to escort you to Almack's this evening."

Davida was silent for a long moment, wondering how to refuse without insulting him. Her mother, who sat nearby with her tambour frame, rushed into the breech. "How very kind of you, my lord. Our first night there will be much more comfortable with a handsome and popular member as our escort."

Pelham lifted a questioning eyebrow at Davida's silence and her serious look. "Miss Gresham?"

"One of the first rules of the physician is to do no harm. Are you sure it is wise for us to continue this pretend-courtship? For your sake, I fear not."

A stubborn set to his mouth warned her of his determination. "I am not now engaged to Lady Elspeth, so I am free to escort whom I please. It would please me very much to escort you."

Davida sighed and smiled slightly. "If you really think it best. But I . . ."

At this moment, Lord Threlbourne was announced.

He was one of the young men Pelham had introduced her to during their drive in the park.

"Gil, why are you plaguing Miss Gresham at this hour," Pelham joked as he shook hands with the gangling viscount.

Threlbourne flushed under his mass of freckles until his face was almost as red as his hair, but he stood his ground. "Miss Gresham wanted to see the Elgin marbles again. You know I can't stay away."

"As much as you like antiquities, you ought to go to Greece. In fact, why don't you start right now. I wanted to take Miss Gresham for a drive."

"Not me! After hearing about the hardships of travel that Hobbhouse and Byron experienced, I'll just let others bring its treasures to me, thank you. But come, Miss Gresham. We must be off."

Threlbourne hastened Davida into the foyer and helped her into her pelisse. It was an overcast, rather cool day, threatening rain, so she accepted the umbrella which Perry gravely offered her.

"Shouldn't let this ham-handed fellow drive you, you know," Pelham called after them as she was handed up into the viscount's high-perch phaeton.

Davida grinned down at him. "I've heard his grays beat your bays in a certain race, however."

Pelham made a fist and banged the wheel as Threlbourne laughed. "It wasn't a fair race. I had a passenger and Gil didn't."

"Then we must have a rematch, Monty. I know, I'll take along Miss Gresham as ballast."

"Well, I like that," Davida choked out over her laugh.

"No, it's not safe for her. You're too cow-handed. We'll race without passengers and then we'll see.

"You're on." Threlbourne pumped his hand. "Name the time."

As Threlbourne mounted the carriage beside her and gave his impatient grays the office to start, Davida's excited voice carried back to Pelham. "Are you really going to race? I should so like to see it."

Pelham smiled to himself as he watched them drive away. He couldn't imagine Elspeth entering so enthusiastically into such a venture. *Davida is up to every rig*, he thought. *A pity Elspeth can't have a bit of her adventurous spirit.*

Chapter Five

For her debut at Almack's, Davida was careful to dress demurely in a pale shade of pink. When she came downstairs, her father approvingly examined her frothy, high-waisted gown of pink lace over a white satin slip. It was cut lower in the front than the gown she had worn to the Stanhope ball, and Davida felt just a bit self-conscious at the swell of bosom it revealed. She wondered if her father would order her upstairs to find a more modest dress.

Sir Charles seemed undisturbed, however. He kissed her cheek and handed her a small, narrow box, a sly grin on his face.

"Carved coral—carved into roses! They're exquisite!" she exclaimed, drawing the necklace from the satin lining. Excitedly she let her father replace the pearls she had donned earlier with the brilliant coral necklace, since she had put matching coral earrings in her ears.

The pier glass in the hall armoire told her that this touch of vivid color greatly enhanced her looks. She was hugging her father with gratitude when Lord Pelham was admitted by a footman.

A look full of approval on his face, Pelham came to her side after greeting her parents. "Trés charmante," he murmured, bending over her gloved hand. For the first time he let his lips lightly caress her fingertips, and Davida gave a jump as that slight touch rocked her senses. Her wide, startled eyes met his, and the look there perplexed her, being rather knowing and speculative.

"It is a nasty night out, be sure you are well covered," he admonished as the ladies' cloaks were brought. Her father, feeling them adequately escorted, was not accompanying them. He knew that he had served her cause well at the Stanhopes' ball. Tonight he looked forward to an evening of card-playing at Boodles, his preferred club, where the stakes were not too high.

The rain couldn't dampen Davida's excitement, nor could her first glimpse of Almack's. She knew it was famous more for the people who came there than for its decor or refreshments, both Spartan at best. But it was the exclusive marriage mart for the *ton,* and she was frankly delighted to finally become one of its prizes. In fact, her need to find an acceptable husband for herself somehow seemed more urgent than ever when she was in the company of the handsome, charming, but unfortunately unavailable Lord Pelham.

It was very pleasant to find that she knew many of the young people there, at least slightly, mostly from her brief acquaintance with Pelham. Even more pleasant was it to find that she was greeted cordially by all, and with enthusiasm by some.

Sarah was there before them and greeted her joyfully. "Davida, you look marvelous," she whispered. "I love the necklace. Is it new?"

"Yes, Papa gave it to me tonight."

"It's very wicked for lovely ladies to whisper secrets," Arnold Lanscombe objected as he lifted Davida's dance card from her hand. Arnold was correctly attired for the evening in the de rigeur knee britches, white tie, and black long-tailed dress coat. But ordinarily he was outrageously dressed in the dandy mode, complete with wild colors and shirt points so high and stiffly starched that he couldn't turn his head.

He had chanced to call one afternoon when her father

was in the drawing room, and Sir Charles had been forced to leave, as he explained later, or he would have laughed in Lanscombe's face.

"Don't give that fribble a second thought," her father had warned her. It cost Davida no pain to assure him she would not.

"I say, no fair, Pelham." Lanscombe used his quizzing glass to examine the dance card. "Down for two already."

Davida reclaimed her card, and, after perusing it, shook her head. "One of them is a waltz."

Pelham lifted his eyebrow in that challenging way that he had. "The waltz was approved by the patronesses last year."

"I can't waltz. That is, I haven't been given permission yet," Davida admitted, feeling more disappointed than she wanted to be. "I shouldn't like to ask on my very first evening."

Pelham only laughed. "A minor obstacle, Miss Gresham. I won't mind asking at all, and I am sure I can obtain permission for you."

When he got that self-assured note in his voice, Pelham seemed to Davida to be older than his twenty-five years, and she was reminded that here was no ordinary young man, but a peer of the realm, with responsibilities to help rule his country as well as to manage his lands and other investments. And how handsome he looked tonight in his stark black-and-white evening clothes, the knee breeches displaying strong, well-developed legs, and the long-tailed coat admirably tailored to display his broad shoulders.

Suddenly Davida frankly yearned to waltz with him, to be close to him and feel his hands on her for those few short, delicious minutes. The strength of her feelings was unexpected and unwelcome, and she exerted herself to direct her attention away from Lord Pelham, an intention difficult to carry out because he seemed determined to distinguish her with his interest. With a pang she realized all of this attention was for the sake of observers who would report his attentiveness to his true love.

Lady Elspeth Howard made a late entrance, very near the time when the doors to Almack's would be firmly shut to all comers, no matter how distinguished. Davida knew the instant she arrived by the change in Lord Pelham, who had not quite succeeded in hiding the fact that he was watching for her appearance.

They were standing in a set to begin a country dance when Davida saw him look over her right shoulder and light up with pleasure. A slight turn of her head and she could see the Howards entering, escorted by Lord Whitham.

She glanced back and saw that Pelham had spotted Whitham, too. His face grew dark with anger. As their turn came to go down the dance, Davida asked him, "Is that not the same young man who was driving her in the curricle that day when . . . ?"

"Yes," snapped Pelham. "Stuffed shirt. Prosy bore. What can she see in him?"

"Smile while you rave, Lord Pelham, or she will see your heart on your sleeve again," Davida told him.

Pelham glared at her for a second and then laughed. They were separated by the dance, but when they came together again, he thanked her. "I shall be merry as a grig. I won't be caught wearing the willow for any woman!"

"That's more like it." Davida gave his hand an encouraging squeeze as they went down the dance again, and he rewarded her with a brilliant smile that caused her heart to give a sudden lurch.

Her next partner was Threlbourne, who frowned at the strains of the minuet. "That fusty old dance. I feel a right fool mincing about like that!"

"Let's promenade, then," Davida suggested. "I wouldn't mind some lemonade, however warm it may be."

Threlbourne quickly organized their refreshments and then led her to a grouping of young people who also appeared to disdain the minuet. It included Elspeth, Whitham, Sarah, and several others Davida did not know. One of these, a tall blond man as handsome as a Greek god, turned and clapped his strong hand on Threlbourne's shoulder as they approached. "I shall even invite Gilbert, if he'll introduce me to this lovely lady he's escorting." The look the Adonis was giving her was both assessing and approving.

"Curzon! They let you in here? Shan't introduce a loose fish like you to such a proper young lady."

"Never mind, do it myself. Harrison Curzon at your service." He made an elaborate leg and then gave Davida a look so warm it put her to the blush.

"I shouldn't reward such boldness, but I suppose I can trust the patronesses not to admit you if you are too dangerous to know. I'm Davida Gresham." She sketched him a curtsy, dropping her eyes in embarrassment at his avid gaze.

"Too dangerous to know! That's what Caro Lamb said of Byron. I promise you, Miss Gresham, I do not aspire to emulate *that* creature." He turned back to her escort. "Tell you what—I'll invite you along anyway, Threlbourne, if you'll promise to bring Miss Gresham."

"Invite me where? What's up?"

"Oh, Elspeth and Harry were just saying how boring all these balls and routs were becoming," Sarah interjected. "Harry is getting up a picnic on his parents' grounds at Elmwood, as a change of pace."

The minuet had just ended, and Pelham had strolled casually up to the group, his partner, Mary Hollings, on his arm. "A picnic? Sure to rain on any day on which *you* plan a picnic, Harry."

"No, Monty, with Lady Elspeth giving it her blessing, it wouldn't dare."

Elspeth smiled and looked enticingly at Pelham. "Of

course it wouldn't. Do say you'll join us, Monty, Mary. Everyone is coming."

Pelham moved to her side. "Picnics aren't exactly in my line, but I could be convinced."

Elspeth looked up at him, and Davida felt a tightening in her chest that constricted her breathing. What a lovely picture they made, both so young and attractive, looking admiringly into each other's eyes.

"I say, do you feel somewhat *de trop*?" Threlbourne drawled to the company at large. Knowing chuckles answered him as the group broke up, leaving Pelham and Elspeth standing together.

Threlbourne returned her to her mother, chatting amiably. When she turned, she realized that Harrison Curzon had followed them. He allowed himself to be introduced to her mother and then turned to her, eyes of ice blue compelling her attention. "Miss Gresham, do you consider our impromptu introduction sufficient grounds to grant me a dance?" He held out his hand hopefully for her dance card.

Davida accepted with pleasure. He was the first young man other than Pelham who could make her heart race with a smile and put her to the blush with a look. Furthermore, there was something very particular in his manner toward her that was encouraging.

She knew who he was, of course. Who did not? The handsome blond could hardly move without his actions being reported in the newspapers. His father was a mere baronet for life, but as wealthy as the Golden Ball, it was said. If he wanted a hereditary title, all he had to do was loan Prinny more money. Harrison Curzon was considered one of the prizes on the marriage mart. At thirty, he was believed to be seriously looking for a wife, too.

Davida's pleasure in his interest was inexplicably washed away in the next instant when she saw Pelham and Elspeth waltzing together. It was the first waltz, the one he'd claimed he would dance with her.

Davida was not one to allow herself the megrims. She threw herself into light flirtations with the several young men who had gathered around her and Sarah as they waited out the forbidden waltz.

The dance Curzon had claimed turned out to be a boulanger. Davida was quite a good dancer and was pleased to find Curzon willing to attempt the showy, difficult dance. They spurred each other on, it seemed, as both grew very inventive with their steps. When it was over, they almost collapsed on each other, laughing.

"This is no dance for the faint of heart," Davida gasped.

"No, indeed, nor for the shy, retiring type either." Curzon smiled in appreciation of his partner.

"Are you suggesting that I am bold, sir?" Davida was just sufficiently touchy on the subject of her behavior to be nettled. She plied her fan with rather more vigor than the heat of the room required, giving Curzon a challenging glance over the gilded ivory tips.

"No more than is pleasing. I find little enjoyment in the company of shrinking violets."

Curzon's icy blue eyes seemed to darken as he looked down at her. "I hope you won't mind if I tell you that you are quite the most attractive creature to grace Almack's this season. Will you do me the honor of driving out with me tomorrow?"

Davida trembled a little at the warmth of that look, which seemed to suggest something far more improper than a drive. "I regret that I am promised tomorrow, Mr. Curzon."

"Then the day after or the day after! Please, my life ceases to have meaning until you name the day." He accompanied his words with an extravagantly prayerful gesture and twinkling eyes.

She smiled and cut her eyes up at him. "Well, then, I believe your life must be quite meaningless until Monday."

"So cruel, and yet so kind." He raised her hand to his lips and then surrendered her reluctantly to her next partner.

Davida was in such a whirl of partners and dances that she quite forgot Pelham until the strains of a waltz again relegated her to the sidelines. Then she saw him bearing down on her, purpose in his stride.

"This nonsense must stop," he asserted, taking her hand and placing it on his arm before leading her across the room so quickly she almost had to run to keep up. Their destination was Lady Jersey, who looked at both of them with teasing eyes as she acknowledged Pelham's bow. "What do you want, Monty, as if I didn't know?"

"Really!" Princess Esterhazy eyed them with disfavor. " 'Tis only her first visit to Almack's. You shouldn't even ask."

"Nonsense," Lady Jersey responded. "She's a sensible, prettily behaved gel, and Monty is . . ."

"A pet of yours," the Princess snapped.

"Yes, he is." Lady Jersey's eyes were warm as she looked at Lord Pelham in a way that suddenly made Davida uncomfortable. Hadn't she heard whispers about Lady Jersey's fondness for younger men?

But in a second the look had changed to one of amused toleration. "Do go on and dance and stop hanging about, children."

Pelham smiled and bowed slightly before turning and sweeping Davida onto the floor, which was already crowded with swiftly moving couples.

It was Davida's first waltz with anyone other than her dancing master or her father. It took her several moments to settle into the rhythm of the music, to relax and begin moving as one with Pelham. She found the sensation of being so close to him both unnerving and delicious.

When she finally felt she had herself in hand, she dared to look at him. He was not very much taller than

she. It seemed to her as she lifted her face that all he
would have to do would be to bend his head slightly and
he could kiss her quite easily.

This disquieting thought caused her to gasp and miss
her step. Pelham had been gazing into the middle distance, a vague smile on his lips. Now he glanced down.
"Did I step on your toes?" he asked, concerned.

"Oh, no, my lord. I just misstepped." She was
painfully aware of his closeness, his hand on her waist.
A blush threatened, and she forced herself into conversation to keep from making a cake of herself. It would
never do for Pelham to guess how attracted she was to
him. Remembering that look he had given her when he
kissed her hand in the foyer, she wondered if he already
knew.

"It has been a delightful evening for me. How about
you, my lord. Has all gone well?"

The cobalt eyes looked affectionately down at her.
"Famously. Elspeth practically asked me to escort her to
Curzon's picnic. And we waltzed together. Oh!" Sud-
denly aware of his failed promise, he apologized.

"Do not think of it. After all, that is what we had
hoped for. I'm so pleased. Soon you'll be engaged again,
no doubt."

"I hope so. And you seem to have attracted a very eligible *parti*."

All innocence, she batted her eyelashes at him.
"Whom do you mean, my lord? I've danced with so
many this evening."

"I think you know, minx! And please stop 'my lord-
ing' me. My friends call me Monty."

"If you will call me Davida."

"I mayn't call you 'Davie,' as Sarah does?" Mischief
lit up his face.

"Only in private, my—ah, Monty. It is a family name,
and my mother would get into a pucker if everyone
began calling me that."

"Agreed."

A comfortable silence fell between them for several moments. Then Pelham cleared his throat. "Should warn you, Davie—Curzon does not have a spotless reputation where women are concerned. Mean to say, hear he's looking for a wife now, but do watch your step there."

Alarmed, Davida lifted her head. "What . . . what do you mean?"

Monty frowned down at her, wondering suddenly why he had said such a thing. Curzon was no more likely than any other gentleman of the *ton* to take advantage of a gently raised, marriageable miss. But now he'd put his foot in it! He'd have to explain.

"Don't fly up into the boughs. I shouldn't have said anything. It's just that young women sometimes become quite hen-witted around him. He has been known to take advantage occasionally of the female's susceptibility to rich and handsome young men."

Davida shook her head. "A young woman's reputation is all to her, Monty. Perhaps I shouldn't go driving with him on Monday as I said I would."

"Don't cry off. I didn't mean to alarm you so. If you behave as you ought, I'm sure he'll do the same."

Davida, somewhat piqued, snapped, "I thank you for the warning. I am accustomed to behaving as I ought, but I will be most circumspect in my dealings with him."

"Yes, I believe you will. You are awake on all suits, Davie." He studied her profile as she turned her head, a slight frown creasing her forehead. A sudden, unexpected feeling of tenderness surged through him. She was really a lovely girl, vivacious and good-natured. He felt compelled to add, "The man who wins you will be fortunate indeed, my girl."

Somewhat mollified, Davida thanked him, firmly suppressing a wish that he would not be quite so complacent about the thought of another man winning her.

Lady Howard's party left early, her daughter Elspeth

once more on the arm of Lord Whitham. It was clear that the pleasure had gone out of the evening for Pelham when they left, yet he continued to dance and laugh and do the pretty for Davida. When the ball began to break up, she was exhausted and more than ready to leave.

They emerged into a thick mist and Pelham moaned, "Hope it doesn't continue to rain like this."

As she followed her mother into the carriage, Davida quizzed him. "Surely you don't doubt your beloved's ability to conjure up a sunny sky for the picnic next week?"

"If she enlists the bishop's assistance, I doubt it very much. Her father's prayers are so long-winded the Almighty would do just the opposite of what he asked, out of irritation."

Davida giggled, but her mother glared at her. "I cannot like this conversation, children. It borders on the sacrilegious."

"Your pardon, ma'am." Pelham looked contrite, but when Davida, her mirth suppressed behind her fan, caught his eye, he winked at her.

As she slowly relaxed into sleep in the early hours of the morning, Davida had a wonderful sense of anticipation. Social ruin had been averted. Her debut at Almack's had been a success; she had met many young men whom her father could only be pleased to have court her. Which of them would call on her tomorrow? Would one of them make her feel as happy inside as that auburn-haired rascal she had helped to win back his true love?

Chapter Six

"So this Curzon, you say, is a baronet's son?"

"Yes, Papa, though only for life. And so handsome. He is tall and blond. Surely the Vikings must have looked something like that. Or perhaps the Greek gods."

Davida felt it necessary to build up her father's interest in Mr. Curzon, because he had been quite disappointed when she told him Lord Pelham and Lady Elspeth seemed to be making it up between them.

"You shall meet him, and no doubt many others. I hardly sat out a dance, and you know most of them will call today." They were at the breakfast table, though it was nearly noon. It had taken Davida quite a long time to become accustomed to town hours, but she had been so tired that sleeping late had been easy this morning.

"Yes, I saw the drawing room was filling up with flowers already." Her father smiled, pleased with his daughter's obvious success.

It was as she predicted. Their drawing room was the scene of constant coming and going well into the afternoon. Invitations piled up on the silver tray in the foyer, and bouquets almost crowded them out of the drawing room.

After the last caller had departed, Davida's mother exclaimed in pleasure, "Such good fortune that Pelham took you up before your come-out ball, dear. We shall make a much better showing now you are becoming acquainted with the *ton*."

Davida held the stack of invitations to her breast,

smiling dreamily. "Yes, now it will be a squeeze. I hope
the duke doesn't mind." It had long been planned that
Sarah's father would come up to London and open his
town mansion for the come-out ball which his daughter
and Davida were going to share. Neither Lady D'Alatri
nor the Greshams had facilities for a large ball.

"I'm sure he'll be very pleased. He was well aware
that Sarah had no intentions of making a push to meet a
great many young men. Now she will have to, whether
she wants to or not."

Lady Sarah had come to London for the season very
reluctantly, for she had long ago determined to wed a
neighbor, Gregory Allensby. He was a serious young
man who had inherited his family's estate early. He bent
all his energies on managing it to the benefit of his
mother and siblings. The duke had no real objection to
Allensby, but wished his daughter to have a wider acquaintance before settling on a husband.

Davida chuckled at her friend's poorly disguised strat-
agems to avoid attracting eligible gentlemen. One of
them had been to set the ball very late in the season, sup-
posedly to give them time to widen their acquaintance.
In truth she was, as Pelham had suggested, reluctant to
be noticed, but now she would possibly find their ball
one of the events of the season!

"But whatever shall we do? We can't possibly attend
all of these." Davida made a helpless gesture with the
pile of invitations.

"Of course not. Now we can be very selective. But we
must try to attend as many as possible. Not much time is
left, if you are to choose a husband this year. Oh, my
dear, Mr. Curzon was very warm in his attentions to you
this afternoon, wasn't he?"

"Yes, he was," Davida replied. She was not truly a shy
person, but with her high coloring she blushed easily,
and Harrison Curzon had put her to the blush more than
once this afternoon with his fulsome compliments and

admiring looks. She guessed he took a mischievous pleasure in her embarrassment.

"A handsome young man, as you said," her father
drawled.

"Yes, but I cannot like him."

"Mama!" Davida turned, astonished, to see her mother
looking unusually stern.

"I can't help it. I don't know why, but I cannot. There
is something so bold about his manner. Almost insolent.
I do not think he would make a comfortable husband."

"Codswallop!" Her father was aghast. "An eligible
parti, and clearly interested. Woman, what kind of a start
is this?"

Her mother rose and walked agitatedly around the
room. "He is not at all as kind as Lord Pelham, I am
sure."

"Your daughter has seen fit to throw Pelham away,
so . . ."

"Papa! He was never mine to . . ."

"Let us not quarrel." Her mother turned to face them.
"Davida is right. Pelham was in alt when Lady Elspeth
took him up again. However we might prefer him as a
son-in-law, he is out of reach. All I am asking is that we
keep our wits about us. You wouldn't want Davida to
choose unwisely and be unhappy."

Her father went to his wife and pulled her into his
arms. "Of course not, my dear. Be assured I will look
over any potential husbands very carefully."

Davida felt a little teary, watching them. In spite of
her father's ambitions, they really did have her best interests at heart. She joined them, hugging them both.
"You are surely the best parents a girl could have."

But as she mounted the stairs to change into a carriage
dress for the ride in the park she had promised Sir Ralph
Moreston, Davida felt weighed down with the pressure
of the necessity to make such a lifelong commitment in a
few short weeks. Her own inclination was to relax and

let matters turn out as they might. Surely eighteen was too young to worry about being on the shelf? But she must please not only herself but her dear parents as well, so she firmly took herself in hand and prepared to continue her search.

She donned her plainest carriage dress, a dark blue bombazine trimmed with white Spanish puffs at the hem and along the sleeves. She did not really like Sir Ralph very much and had no wish to entice him with one of her more fetching costumes.

Unfortunately Sir Ralph was a favorite of her father, who had met him at the Stanhope ball. "Sir Ralph Moreston, eh! Good man, good man," he boomed approvingly when he heard who her escort was. "Waterloo hero, very sound Tory. A very solid man indeed, Davida."

It was an unfortunate choice of words. Davida giggled behind her fingers. "Very solid indeed, Papa. He must weigh above twenty stone!"

"Now, not all men can look like your blond Adonis. He'd make you a fine husband. You'd be a lady . . ."

"Yes, Papa," she sighed, turning to pat her curls into place beneath her untrimmed bonnet as Perry admitted the portly baronet. He greeted her father effusively, then eyed Davida with delight.

"Lovely, lovely! Not all decked out with frills and furbelows like so many flighty misses. Plain and sensible."

Their drive was not a success from Davida's standpoint. After seating her in his rather ancient barouche, Sir Ralph spent all of his time disparaging the expense and frivolity around him. "Spending all they have to cut a dash. Fribbles!" He saw Davida eyeing a handsome team of grays that flashed past them. "And those mettlesome animals they dash about town with—dangerous business. You never need worry that my team will bolt with us, Miss Gresham."

Davida bit the inside of her cheek to keep from laugh-

ing. Except for their docked tails and braided manes, Sir
Ralph's stolid team would have looked right at home behind a plow. Whatever her father thought of the man, she
found him a pompous bore, as well as unattractive. She
politely refused his offer to take her to an improving lecture during the next week, and escaped into her home
with great relief when the drive was over.

No more successful was her ride with Arnold
Lanscombe the next morning. She had allowed the
dandy to provide her with a mount in spite of her father's dislike of him, for they had not brought any saddle
horses with them to London, and she missed riding
sorely.

But the mount Lanscombe provided was disappoint-
ing, a placid gelding with ears so large she wondering if
he might be a mule. Lanscombe was little better
mounted. Obviously all of his energy and treasure went
into his clothing.

Indeed, once he had induced her to comment upon his
riding jacket, which was mustard-colored with sienna
trim and sported the largest buttons Davida had ever
seen, he spent the rest of their time together commenting
upon the clothing and equipage of those around them.
Davida did not know if her green riding habit met with
his approval, and did not care. She escaped from him at
the end of the ride with as much relief as from her outing
with Sir Ralph.

The most acceptable of her escorts that week was
Gilbert, Viscount Threlbourne. She did not particularly
admire his looks, but he had an easy, kindly manner and
lively personality that she enjoyed. It was very clear
early on, however, that he was not courting her. Indeed,
he had spend a goodly portion of their first drive telling
her about his cousin Virginia, just now out of the school-
room, with whom he had an understanding.

Although both families actively encouraged the
match, her parents thought her too young to marry, and

he agreed. "Let her have a season next year, and then we can begin to plan our wedding," he confided. The tone of his voice more than anything he said made Davida believe that he was very attached to his young cousin. She told him quite honestly that she thought he'd make an admirable husband and that Virginia was very fortunate to have attracted his interest.

By the time of their drive on Monday, it was clear to Davida that Harrison Curzon was the most interesting of her beaus. It was equally clear that Curzon was a serious suitor. He visited every afternoon that they were at home, reluctantly parting after staying the accepted fifteen minutes each time. He made it a point to know which entertainments she was attending in the evenings and quickly appeared at her side wherever she went. He always claimed two dances and virtually insisted on one of them being a waltz.

Unlike Sir Ralph and Arnold Lanscombe, he could converse without criticizing all around him, and was an amusing partner for the dances they shared. She found herself looking forward to their drive, when she might have the opportunity to know him better.

Davida was definitely drawn to him, though honesty forced her to admit to herself that she felt nowhere near the attraction to him that she felt for Pelham. But Pelham had not called on her again. When they came across one another in the social whirl, he was friendly, but he was obviously busy courting Elspeth. Each day she read the newspapers avidly, expecting an announcement of the renewal of their engagement, but as yet none had appeared.

Curzon claimed her for their drive in the park with a very possessive air and made Davida not a little uncomfortable by taking her hand and pulling the glove down to press a kiss on her wrist before he helped her into his curricle.

Her pink-cheeked silence seemed to amuse him as he expertly flicked his cattle into a trot. "Cat got your tongue, Miss Gresham?" he chuckled. Why did men seem to enjoy putting women out of countenance, Davida wondered.

"Your blacks are very showy, Mr. Curzon, with their matching white stockings. However did you find such nearly identical horses?"

Her diversionary gambit seemed to work. With the enthusiasm of the true horseman, he informed her, "Believe it or not, they were both bred on my father's stud in Lancashire. They are about a year apart in age and from the same sire."

"And the entirely black curricle—all very impressive."

"And now the ensemble is complete, with a black-haired beauty by my side." He arched a brow at her, the vivid, almost piercing ice blue eyes reminding her somehow of a bird of prey.

"Are they fast, Mr. Curzon? Have you raced them?"

"Do you find my gallantries unpleasant, Davida?" His free hand reached over to cover hers, which were tightly clenched in her lap.

"Oh, no! I suppose I just haven't yet quite learned how to flirt properly." She opened her eyes wide, trying to look as naive as possible.

"Nonsense. You are a born flirt. What is throwing you is that you know I am serious, is that not so?" The intentness of his look disconcerted her.

At that moment Davida noticed that they were not on the right road to Hyde Park. "Where are we going, please?" She tried to control the nervous tremor in her voice.

"Don't be alarmed." He released her hand. "I am just going to drive in Green Park. It will not be as crowded at this hour, and we can be more private. Does that distress you?" There was genuine concern in his voice and doubt in his eyes. "You don't suspect me of having dishonorable intentions toward you, do you, Davida?"

"Green Park will be quite satisfactory, Mr. Curzon." She chose to ignore the question of his intentions, but Pelham's warning was, she realized, coloring her behavior toward her handsome blond suitor.

Davida was silent as Curzon concentrated on tooling his blacks through the busy London streets. She admired good driving and took pleasure in seeing the skill with which he handled the ribbons.

When they turned into the park, he slowed the pace and turned to Davida, transferring the reins to his right hand. He slid his left arm around her and pulled her against him. "How I long to kiss you, Davida. It's not possible here, but we can be a little closer, at least."

Astonished by his boldness, she looked hastily around to see if anyone was near enough to know what he had done. The feel of his strong, hard body beside hers startled her. It wasn't an entirely disagreeable sensation, this proximity to a powerful male body, which surely intensified the impropriety of the experience! She tried to wiggle free, but his firm grasp easily prevented her.

"Please, Mr. Curzon. I have done nothing to encourage such familiarity."

The broad brow wrinkled, the icy eyes narrowed. "I know you are a proper young lady, but I do not believe you are cold. You *are* aware that I am courting you in form and in earnest, are you not?"

"This is beyond . . ." she began, but his voice cut across hers, harsh with emotion.

"Now, Davida, tell me who my rival is? I thought at first Pelham, but he is entirely taken up with the self-righteous if delectable Lady Elspeth. I really can't credit that you have a *tendre* for Threlbourne or Lanscombe, and if I am not very much mistaken, you actively dislike Sir Ralph Moreston."

"What makes you think . . . that is, I have a great many

gentleman friends, but no one in particular. And . . . and
I beg leave to tell you I did not give you permission to
use my first name!" Davida was beginning to feel
trapped, and her instinct was to fight.

The curricle was barely moving. Curzon turned toward her, loomed over her, it almost seemed, his hawk's
eyes intent upon her. "My suit displeases you?"

"You go too fast. I've only known you since Wednesday."

He studied her narrowly, and Davida met his gaze
squarely, almost defiantly, her usually rosy cheeks flam-
ing now in agitation.

After what seemed to Davida an interminable time,
Curzon's features softened into a smile and he released
his hold on her. "Very well. Forgive me if I've ben precipitate in my lovemaking. I'll woo you slowly and gently, as you deserve. Unless you wish me to desist
entirely?"

Davida dropped her glance and fiddled with her reticule. "No, of course not. I . . . just wish to be very
sure . . ."

"That does you credit, my dear. If you only knew how
many young women have been so determined to wed my
gold that no insult, no impropriety was serious enough to
discourage them!"

"So you have become accustomed to being able to behave toward my sex in an insulting, improper manner."
Davida frowned at him fiercely.

"If I have, you have certainly given me a salutary set-
down today! May we cry friends?"

"Of course." Davida answered his beguiling smile
with a hesitant one.

"Then let me give you a hint of what these blacks can
do, *Miss* Gresham!" So saying, he flicked the pair into a
spanking pace that fairly took her breath away. She lifted
her face to the wind and laughed joyfully. A devilish
grin lit his face as he observed her delight in their speed.

When he pulled them into a cooling walk, Davida clapped her hands in delight. "They are marvelous. And you are an excellent whipster. I wonder . . . ?"

"Yes?" He was smiling broadly in obvious enjoyment of her excitement.

"Pelham and Threlbourne spoke of having raced. They are planning a rematch, but I suspect these beauties could take either of their pair."

"I think they could, too. Perhaps we'll put it to the touch at the picnic?"

"Famous!" Davida's eyes glowed with excitement. She rode home in perfect charity with Harrison Curzon, even agreeing to accompany him to a private viewing of the Royal Academy's exhibition on the following morning. Still, she was determined that he would only kiss the tips of her fingers when he took her hand to bid her farewell.

He smiled wickedly up at her as he bent over her stiff, unyielding little hand. "At least you are not unaware of me, my dear, and so sweetly proper, *Miss* Gresham." He stepped away and waved jauntily as he dashed down the steps.

Watching him go, Davida felt a little twinge of guilt over the way she had answered his questions. She had given him the impression that she hadn't a *tendre* for anyone, but she knew that wasn't true. However, her interest in Pelham was hopeless, so there was no reason to reject Curzon out of hand.

He was eligible in every way, although, like her mother, she found him difficult to be comfortable with. But that might pass on better acquaintance. Truly eligible suitors were not so thick upon the ground as to be dismissed lightly. Yes, she would continue to see him, but after their brief contretemps in the park, she would take care not to encourage him too much until she knew her own mind better.

Chapter Seven

As they drove along the Strand toward the Royal Academy at Somerset house the following morning, Davida learned that just as Pelham was an amateur musician who took his music seriously, Curzon was an amateur painter who took painting very seriously indeed. He explained that he was a member of the Academy, one of a very few talented amateurs allowed to belong to the country's foremost professional society for the training and promotion of artists. It was as a member that he was able to invite her to view the paintings privately.

Finding that Davida was relatively ignorant about the Academy, for she was definitely not an artist, her escort proudly and knowledgeably gave her a thumbnail sketch of its origins and functions. "Oddly enough, it traces its beginnings to the Foundling Hospital chartered in 1739. Hogarth was one of many wealthy and influential people who joined the crown in supporting this worthy cause."

"You mean *the* Hogarth, who did the superb satirical cartoons?"

"The same. He was one of the original governors. He began the practice of donating works to the hospital and encouraged other artists to do so."

"Like his satires?"

"No, Hogarth was a master painter, as well as a satirist. His first donation was a portrait of the founder of the hospital. Other artists followed suit, making similar donations."

Davida clapped her hands. "Let me guess. Before long, people were visiting the hospital for the sake of the paintings."

Curzon nodded his approval of her quick comprehension. "And paying for the privilege. After Hogarth's death many other artists continued the tradition. The success of these exhibitions led to dreams of a separate academy for training artists and exhibiting their works."

"What an odd way for a school of art to begin."

"A great deal of the credit goes to our old king, who lent the project his support. He was healthy then. Poor old farmer George!"

With enthusiasm and a range of knowledge that indicated that Curzon was also well versed in architecture, he pointed out to her the salient features of the fine building which housed the Royal Academy: its Corinthian columns and pilasters, balustrades, decorated windows, and other ornamentations designed to give it beauty and dignity.

It was with a new appreciation that Davida entered through the two-story Corinthian columns into the imposing vestibule. She had been to the exhibition before, of course, but the crush of the crowd had prevented her from truly enjoying the paintings, much less the architecture of the building.

Instead of proceeding up the grand staircase to the exhibition rooms, as she had on previous visits, Davida was led to the right, past the porter's lodge and into the Life School, a commodious room full of artists' easels and various props and draperies. The strong scent of oil paints permeated the room.

Curzon pointed out several long wires hanging from the ceiling, ending in loops or hooks. "What do you think those are for, Miss Gresham?"

Davida wrinkled her nose in concentration, but couldn't come up with an intelligent guess. Mischief lit her eyes. "Instruments of torture, perhaps?"

On a shout of laughter he led her to the raised stage over which these hooks dangled. "Perhaps our models sometimes think so, but they are really intended to assist them."

"Do explain, Mr. Curzon," Davida urged impatiently, her curiosity aroused.

Instead of explaining, he led her to a position beneath one and gave it a tug. It lowered to about his shoulder. He reached forward and took her wrist and placed it in the curve of the hook. "Now do you see?"

A little uneasily, Davida watched him maneuver another hook. "Not entirely." She resisted his attempt to place her other wrist in it, and he did not insist, but stood back, looking at her intently. At last Davida comprehended, and she struck a pose, using the hook to hold her wrist before herself in a dramatic gesture.

"Exactly! They help our models maintain gravity-defying poses for long periods of time."

"You speak of 'our' models."

"Yes, I have the privilege of attending the life classes. Mind, I pay well for the privilege, but it is worth every farthing to be able to draw the human form unfettered by clothing."

At this Davida felt her coloring beginning to heighten, and she lifted her arm free of the hook. She was further discomposed by Curzon's next statement.

"How I should like to paint you, Davida. If I only could capture that devastating mixture of white and rose that is your coloring!" It seemed to her that he was undressing her with his eyes, and his look had become almost fanatical.

Hastily, Davida murmured, "I think we should go see the exhibition now."

For once it was Curzon who flushed and looked embarrassed. "Forgive me. I always seem to be skirting the edge of propriety with you. And you have made it abundantly clear that you do not like it, have you not, *Miss*

Gresham?" Brows arched, he held out his hand to assist her from the stage. With only a little hesitation, she took it.

It was truly a pleasure to view the exhibition without the crowds that usually attended it. So popular had the Royal Academy's yearly offerings become that in spite of raised fees and attempts to limit viewers to the *beau monde,* sometimes the great hall was so crowded that people had been known to faint.

With only Curzon and the venerable porter accompanying her, their footsteps echoing in the huge room, she admired the crowded floor-to-ceiling mass of paintings. Davida listened with pleasure to Curzon's knowledgeable comments. He especially recommended the paintings of Edwin Landseer, a newcomer to the Academy.

"Truly, I have never enjoyed viewing paintings so much before. I only wish more of them were on eye level. I can scarcely see those near the ceiling."

"Too bad I am not in the habit of carrying a quizzing glass. This would be one occasion on which it might have some useful function." Curzon pantomimed a dandy, imaginary glass held to his twinkling eyes.

Davida grinned at the notion of tall, dignified Harrison Curzon with a quizzing glass. For all of his elegance, there was nothing of the affected about him. Her respect for him deepened as he guided her through the large collection of Old Masters which the Academy had accumulated, enriching her appreciation of them with his knowledgeable comments.

"They are invaluable as a source of study and inspiration for neophyte artists, many of whom do not have entrée into the great houses as you and I do, to see the paintings of the masters."

"I should like to see some of your paintings, Mr. Curzon." Davida asked hesitantly, knowing this was tricky ground. If she truly admired his work there would be no problem. But if she did not, then what? She was not practiced in the art of insincere flattery, yet she did not want to hurt the man's feelings.

"You already have." He smiled triumphantly. "In fact, you admired one."

"I did? When? Which one?"

"I have three in the current exhibition. They are unsigned and not for sale, of course. You liked the one of the young maids trying on their mistress's bonnets."

"That one! Oh, yes, it is wonderful!" Davida was relieved to be able to be completely honest. "But why do you enter them anonymously?"

With a soft, regretful sigh, Curzon explained. "I wish them to be praised or damned on their own merit, not on the basis of my name. And, of course, to sell them would be déclassé."

"I suppose so, but it seems a pity not to sign them."

"Perhaps you will understand why I almost wish they were for sale?"

At her quizzical look he spread his arms resignedly. "If they were sold at a good price, I should have a better sense of my artistic abilities. If something is truly valued, people will pay for it. But I am afraid I am damned to give my works as gifts and always fear they are taken out of hiding and hung just in time for my visits." He tried for an amused, ironic tone, but Davida sensed his vulnerability on this point and had never liked him half so well before.

"I believe I do know how you feel. Whenever I sing in a musicale, and people, particularly young men, praise me to the skies, I never know if their enthusiasm is for my singing, my appearance, or the fact that at last it is over and they can get some refreshments." Curzon chuckled at this, and she smiled wistfully at him. "I have occasionally daydreamed of appearing, disguised of course, in an opera at King's Theatre. Then, if I did not attract oranges, I would know my voice is worthy of praise."

"I assure you I would toss you flowers, not oranges."

"But then, you have never heard me sing, Mr. Curzon."

"And speaking of refreshments . . ."

"Oh, were we?" Her eyes quizzed him merrily.

"If not, perhaps we should. What would you say to sharing some ices with me at Gunther's?"

Davida agreed, but insisted that he point out his other two paintings to her as they left. She was able quite honestly to admire them. Truly Harrison Curzon was a talented artist.

When Davida returned from this outing with Curzon she was quietly but deeply thrilled. She felt she had glimpsed a little of the soul of the man, and she found it compatible with her own.

Also, she was flattered that Curzon had conversed with her in such a manner as indicated he thought she was intelligent, instead of treating her as a child or a lackwit, as so many young men did.

She shared her pleasure with her parents. Her father was enthusiastic, her mother more reserved on learning that Davida had begun to seriously consider Harrison Curzon for a husband.

Montgomery Derwent Villars, fourth Baron Pelham, was perturbed. He ran his hands though his dark auburn curls, destroying what little was left of his valet's efforts to style his hair à la Brutus.

Against the soft murmurs and clinks of glassware of White's at the dinner hour, his oath was explosive, and caused his companion to start and exclaim, "Steady on, old boy. Do you want an audience?" Pelham's dinner partner was a tall, elegantly thin man with very fine brown hair beginning to thin on his forehead. He had a fashionable appearance of world-weariness.

"No, but hang it all, Stanley, I'm tired of being tied in knots by that woman."

Lord Stanley Bede-Holmes, Earl of Carrothers, waved his long, thin hand dismissively. "Then give her up. Lucky for you she cried off."

The thought apparently hadn't entered Pelham's head. He stared, astonished, at his friend. "Give her up? I can't. I love her."

"All right then, out with it. What has she done this time to put you in such a pucker?" Lord Carrothers was seven years Pelham's senior and often stood in the place of an older brother to him. Pelham had been at University with Stanley's younger brother, Edwin, who had been killed at Waterloo.

"She's so starchy and proper. I mean, it was just a kiss. I wasn't going to ravish her. We *are* going to be married, after all. And hang it, she looked so demmed desirable in that gauzy, candy-striped dress."

"So you pulled her into a dark corner at Vauxhall and kissed her. Entirely understandable. Myself, I have never been able to figure out what females expect, when they make themselves so tempting." Carrothers' deep-set brown eyes gave no hint of any intention of irony.

"Exactly!" Pelham lifted his head from his hands. "She stiffened up and pushed me away, and then slapped me. Slapped me, if you can believe it! And not gently, neither. Accused me of treating her like Haymarket ware. And when I told her it was all right, as we were going to be married, she said, 'I shouldn't count on it'!"

Carrothers considered the rare roast of beef steaming on the table before them. "Here, have something to eat. You're going to get bosky if you just drink."

"Feel like getting bosky," Pelham mumbled crossly.

"Well, don't. You can't handle your liquor well, and you know it. Be sick as a dog tomorrow."

"Tomorrow is that blasted picnic. I wonder if she'll still let me drive her?"

"Oh, yes, the famous picnic. Curzon's do, isn't it, to show off the spectacular grounds of Elmwood?"

"Yes, and that's another thing. Curzon and Davida."

Carrothers arched an expressive eyebrow as he forked a succulent bite of roast. "What's wrong? Afraid he'll give your little protégée a slip on the shoulder?"

"He'd damned well better not."

"Well, I shouldn't worry. I think he means to fix his interest there. Heard he'd given his latest bit of muslin, La Desmarest, her *congé*. Told her he was getting married."

Pelham frowned and looked up at the ceiling. "I can't like it."

"Why not?" Stanley's usual imperturbability slipped a bit in astonishment. "Good match for her. Before you took her up she was unknown to the *ton,* and now she's about to land one of the biggest prizes on the marriage mart."

"Is it a good match? Somehow I just don't feel he's right for her. She needs a light hand on the reins. I've known Curzon to treat his women rather roughly."

Stanley's brow arched in surprise. "His lightskirts, hmmm? But not his wife, surely?"

"Perhaps not. But I'd hate to see Davida made unhappy. She's a merry little sprite." Pelham smiled, a warm look in his eyes.

"Umm hmmm? Perhaps you should give up on Lady Elspeth and pursue Miss Gresham. She's a taking little thing, that I'll vouch for." Pelham had introduced Davida to Lord Carrothers at the Stanhope ball, and his friend had been warm in praise of her.

"Oh, don't be ridiculous. We're friends, that's all. She would be astonished if I began to court her. And besides, I love Elspeth."

Carrothers did not challenge this pronouncement. "Then eat some roast beef and recruit your strength for your outing tomorrow. And put that brandy decanter away."

"Softly, Stanley. You aren't my nursemaid."

"No, just your friend."

His steady brown-eyed gaze caused Pelham to drop his eyes to his plate. "Damn it all, do you always have to be right?" Then an idea occurred to him. "Stanley, you liked Davida, didn't you?"

"Told you so. Pleasant and pretty, proper but spirited. Make someone a capital wife."

"That's why I was wondering whether you . . ."

"Someone. Not me. I don't intend to step into the parson's mousetrap for a good many years yet. There are too many lovely cyprians out there, too many lonely wives and widows, to limit my attentions to one woman. Although . . ." A musing tone entered Carrothers' voice as he gazed off in the distance. "Nothing to say a man can't enjoy the muslin company after he gets leg-shackled."

"Forget I hinted. Davida deserves a husband who'll keep his marriage vows."

"Why must you rush into harness, Monty? You're only twenty-five. And don't tell me you need an heir. Your cousin Herbert has two fine boys coming up, and . . ."

"On this subject we never have agreed, Stanley. Don't care for the 'muslin company' business. Never have. My one venture in that direction was disastrous, as you'll recall."

"Monty, Monty, wives can die in childbirth, too."

"But not in shame and fear for their immortal soul. No, after Catherine's death I swore I'd never put another creature in such a situation. She was so frightened, Stanley. Not of dying, but of damnation. But it was me who felt damned, by what I had done to her."

Stanley shifted uncomfortably in his seat. "There are ways to prevent . . ."

"But none are sure. Besides, I want something more from life than these shallow, brief, and tawdry liaisons."

Dryly Stanley intoned, "You and Lady Elspeth are

well suited, then, both as proper as parsons. Come, eat up. I want to be at the theater before the last curtain falls. I have my eye on a little opera dancer, mustn't let anyone else snag her first."

Pelham rolled his eyes. "You and your opera dancers. It's disgusting. A man of your years should be thinking of finding a comfort and helpmeet for his old age."

Brown eyes glinted. "Not quite in my dotage yet. But if I were, assure you I'd find someone older than these eighteen-year-old chits you are agonizing over."

Since Pelham was well aware that Carrothers' seemingly shallow attitudes toward females were to some extent a smoke screen to cover a long-standing and very serious love affair with an older married woman, he discreetly decided to let the subject drop. Instead, he worried his roast while considering what tone to take with Elspeth on the morrow, providing she would condescend to receive him.

Chapter Eight

The day of the picnic dawned as fair as anyone could have wished. The air was a bit brisk, so Davida wore a dark blue pelisse over a light wool carriage dress in her favorite shade of sky blue. To shield her face from the sun she wore a poke bonnet which matched the pelisse, as did the half boots that peeped from beneath her skirt. Gilbert tucked a lap robe around her, his vivid red hair tossed by the wind.

"Hope you shan't be too cold. Mother is one of the chaperons. She's following in the landau if you'd prefer to ride inside."

"Not at all. I'm enjoying the sunshine. And it will doubtless warm up."

At the same time that this scene was taking place, Pelham was tucking a cool, condescending Elspeth into his curricle. He was relieved that she had decided to ride with him, but a little put off by her cold manner. Still, he made her comfortable and whipped up his team.

Davida's prediction of warmer temperatures was justified. By the time the dozen or so carriages and curricles converged on the Curzon family's estate an hour's drive from London, the sun had done its work. She surrendered her pelisse to a footman before joining the group gathering on the steps of the Curzons' stately home.

Her heart did a little flutter dance at the sight of Harrison, looking impossibly handsome in his chocolate brown morning coat and buff inexpressibles. He greeted

Davida warmly, his full lips pressing her fingers firmly through her glove. She lowered her eyes in confusion at her unexpectedly strong reaction to him. Was she perhaps falling in love?

"I need to steal your lovely passenger for a moment, Gil. Know you won't mind." Without waiting for a response, Curzon led Davida away from the little knot of guests standing on the broad marble steps.

"Miss Gresham, I want to introduce you to my grandmother. She's the only one of my family in residence today."

"Oh!" It was so particular, so distinguishing an action that she began to feel rather panicky. She was beginning to have a *tendre* for him, perhaps, but she wasn't ready to consider a declaration. Introducing her to his family seemed ominously close to proposing.

"Do you think we should? I mean, it's not quite fair to your other guests, and besides, I didn't come prepared to . . . I'm rather casually dressed for . . ."

He grinned down at her. "You are adorable when you are flustered. You couldn't look more fetching, and my grandmama is not in the least intimidating. Please come?"

"Very well." She succumbed with good grace, and allowed herself to be led into the vast, elegant entryway of the Curzon mansion. Their steps echoed as he steered her into a formal drawing room dominated by an enormous Adam fireplace carved of white marble. A fire crackled in it in spite of the increasing warmth of the day. In front of it, with a firescreen to protect her, huddled an elderly woman, quite bent with age.

"Grandmama, I would like to make Miss Davida Gresham known to you."

Davida curtsied, and lifted her head to see a pair of shrewd old eyes of the same ice blue as Harrison's "So! You bring a young girl to meet me at last. Blue eyes, porcelain complexion, rosy cheeks. A feast for your artist's eyes, I quite agree. But is there more to her than beauty, I wonder?"

"Much more, Grandmama, as you shall soon have occasion to learn. Unfortunately I have other guests to greet, so we cannot linger."

Davida blushed furiously. She felt like a prime bit of cattle being paraded and discussed before purchase. Still, she murmured a greeting, smiled prettily, and let herself be led away quite as if she had been more honored than annoyed by this encounter.

When all of his guests had arrived, Curzon began to steer them through the formal gardens. "We're going to walk to the picnic site. It is through the woods and on the edge of that lake you can glimpse beyond the trees."

Though some of the young ladies complained about walking, it suited Davida very well. She wanted the opportunity to enjoy the landscaping genius of Capability Brown. She strode out eagerly with Gilbert on one side and Harrison on the other. "You promised us archery, Mr. Curzon. I brought my heavy gloves." She held up her reticule, her sparkling blue eyes challenging him.

"Indeed, my lovely Diana, the targets are already set up."

Just behind them, Elspeth, leaning on Pelham's arm, wrinkled her nose. "I have never felt that archery was a truly ladylike activity myself. The next thing you know, women will begin shooting pistols!"

"I'm afraid I will quite sink myself in your eyes, Lady Elspeth," Davida tossed back over her shoulders, in no way embarrassed. "I dearly love target practice with pistols, though I don't hunt. Papa taught me and says I'm an excellent marksman."

"Are you, indeed?" Curzon frowned. "I am afraid I agree with Lady Elspeth on this. 'Tis most unfeminine, a woman firing a pistol."

Davida tossed her head dismissively. Pelham laughed. "You're only afraid she'd beat you, Curzon. Mean to say, everyone knows you can't hit the target, much less the bulls-eye."

The shout of laughter from several members of the party caused Curzon to smile somewhat ruefully. "A palpable hit, Monty, but spoken by a man who handles a sword like a cricket bat!"

Their banter continued until they reached the beautifully landscaped clearing, where an elaborate feast was set up and waiting for them. Tables, chairs, silver service, champagne, and gourmet delights by the dozens awaited their pallets, served by footmen in handsome livery.

Afterward, a leisurely walk along the lakeshore was generally agreed to be the best assistance in digesting the large repast. Davida found herself walking with Pelham and Threlbourne, Elspeth having rather conspicuously made a bid for Curzon's escort.

As she walked along, Davida's eye was caught by an unusually shaped white rock near the shoreline. She bent to pick it up, and turned its shape over in her hands with pleasure. "Look, Monty, Gil. A trilobite."

"A . . . what?" Gilbert wrinkled his brow in perplexity.

"Why—so it is. But how did you know?" Pelham's amazement was almost comical as he took the object from her and examined it closely.

"Do you think females cannot know about fossils? I have quite a collection of them." Davida retrieved the specimen and dusted it off before dropping it into her reticule.

Since paleontology was one of Pelham's passions, he was eager to hear more, but Elspeth and Curzon had come up behind them. "Fossils! I do not believe in them." Elspeth's voice was shrill. "It is just chance that the rock looks like a living thing. Of course living things can't be turned into stones."

Not wishing to come to cuffs with Elspeth, Davida

turned away. "Well, they're interesting, anyway. What I wouldn't give to see some of the truly amazing finds in America. Have you heard, Monty, of Mr. Benjamin Peale's discovery of the bones of huge animals, larger than the largest elephants. Just imagine! Such beasts must have once walked the earth."

Pelham responded eagerly, "I saw one of the skeletons when he exhibited it here, when I was just a child. It awakened my interest in America's amazing paleontology. Their discoveries have given our taxonomists quite a bit to think about. Are you familiar with Cuvier's . . ."

Curzon interrupted, frowning. "Are you two talking Greek?"

"No!" Elspeth's shrilly indignant voice startled them all. "They are talking heathen. It is sacrilegious and against all Scripture to think that giant animals that no longer exist once roamed the earth."

Pelham turned, obviously goaded by her tone of voice as well as her words. "And pray, Lady Elspeth, how do you account for these complete skeletons of giant animals that have been found?"

"Some natural philosophers think these species lived on the earth before the flood but were wiped out when . . ." Davida began.

But Elspeth, her lovely face distorted with fury, interrupted. "The Devil planted them there as a temptation to those whose pride in their own intellect would lead them into mortal sin."

"Then I confess to being a terrible sinner." Pelham bowed stiffly to her, his face dark with anger.

Elspeth stared at him furiously, and then turned to Curzon. "Give me your arm, Harrison. Let us leave the bluestocking and the atheist to their speculations."

To Davida's surprise, Curzon did as he was asked, casting a dark, angry look at Davida as she stood frozen with shock between Pelham and Threlbourne.

"I say," murmured Gilbert uncomfortably.

After a long moment of silence, Pelham turned and took Davida's arm, leading her in the opposite direction.

"I'm so sorry, Monty," she whispered.

"Don't worry so much about me," he said, smiling and cocking his head. "Unless I miss my guess, you have been damaged a bit, too, Davie."

"Never mind. I am no bluestocking, but if Mr. Curzon can't tolerate a woman with no interests other than gowns and jewelry, it is best we should understand each other before . . ."

He gave her a close look. "By the tone of your voice, I'd guess you are not as indifferent as you allow."

She shook her head sadly. "But my affections are not as engaged as yours are, I don't believe."

"Fortunate girl." Pelham's mouth was set in grim line. They silently returned to the main party, which was congregating around the archery range.

Davida made up her mind to ignore the incident by the lake and enjoy herself, and she did. A lively competition sprang up, and she bested all female rivals and most of the males before losing by a narrow margin to Curzon, who muttered in her ear, "I *think* you did not let me win, my dear."

"It would not be worth my trouble to do so," she snapped, her eyes glittering defiantly.

Curzon's mood had gradually improved during their archery match, and the look he gave her now was admiring. "I like your spirit, Miss Gresham. You do not stoop to truckle, do you?"

She relaxed a little, giving him a tentative smile. "I hope I would never feel the need to do so."

"With me, never." He chucked her under the chin, a broad grin on his handsome face.

As he turned away to accept congratulations on his win and face his remaining opponents, Davida couldn't help but wonder. If he truly felt that way, why had he looked so troubled over the fossil incident? She sighed as she stripped her archery gloves off. Sometimes men were very hard to understand.

When the party drifted back toward the circular drive in front of the mansion, Curzon took note of Threlbourne's high-spirited grays plunging and challenging his tiger for control. He turned suddenly to Pelham, who was stiffly escorting a wooden-faced Elspeth.

"I hear you and Gilbert are planning a rematch of your famous race."

"Oh, yes!" His face lit up. "What say, Gil?"

Gilbert and Davida were following close behind. "Any time, Monty."

"I'd like to test my team against the both of you," Curzon said. "Miss Gresham informs me that she thinks they'd leave you in the dust."

"Never, Davie!" Pelham grinned at her. "Harrison's blacks are just for show."

"Will you put a monkey on that, Pelham?"

"Absolutely. Name the time and place."

Elspeth gasped. "Racing your horses is bad enough, but betting is an abomination."

"Oh, save your puritanical rantings," Pelham snapped. "I'm no gamester, but a friendly wager does no harm."

"Indeed, it does *you* a great deal of harm." Elspeth drew herself up. "I find I do not wish to return to town with so irresponsible an escort. I shall ask Lady Margaret to take me up in her landau."

"As you wish." Pelham bowed stiffly to her and then turned away. "What say, Gilbert? No time like the present. Shall we show Curzon what real horseflesh can do?"

"I'm in, Monty, but not today. Must take Miss Gresham back, don't you know."

"Oh, no, I'd love to watch the race first. But perhaps you shouldn't do it right now, Monty." Her eyes anxiously followed Elspeth's stiff march up the steps of Elmwood.

But other members of the party had heard of the challenge by now and were eagerly urging the race to be held right away.

"Nonsense!" Pelham's eyes flashed defiance. "No reason not to race! No time like the present, is there? What's the best course, Harry?"

Curzon quickly outlined a route for the race, sending a footman pell-mell to tell his grooms to ready his blacks.

The race would begin and end at the gate to the Curzons' long circular drive, so those who chose to observe, which included most of the picnic guests, were able to see them off and wait at the finish line for their return.

Just before he mounted his curricle, Pelham came to Davida. "Well, Davie, since you seem to be the instigator of this race . . ."

She sighed, tears stinging her eyes. "Oh, Monty. I never dreamed the trouble I'd cause you."

"I wasn't going to chastise you. Perhaps I am indebted to you." He glanced toward the mansion, his face thoughtful. "I am quite out of patience with Elspeth. I only wondered if you wished to make a small wager on the outcome?"

Davida laughed away her tears. "Certainly not! Curzon's blacks are true speedsters, but you may be the superior whip, and Gilbert is no sluggard. I'll just cheer you all three on."

He laughed. "Very diplomatic, Davie. But you'll wish you'd laid your blunt on me." He mounted his curricle and drew it alongside the other two. Davida noticed that Curzon was looking back at them, a scowl marring his features. *Now what?* She stared at him in surprise. *He certainly is a moody man.*

The race was hidden from the observers for most of its route, but when they had completed their circuit, they emerged from the trees, charging toward the finish line. Curzon's blacks were just ahead of Pelham's bays, and as they thundered past the cheering group of young people, it was clear that the blacks had won, if only by a nose. Oddly, Lord Threlbourne's carriage was nowhere in sight.

Amid tumultuous cheers the two men jumped from their curricles and tossed the reins to the waiting grooms. The steaming horses were led away to be cooled down as the antagonists clapped one another on the shoulders and turned toward their friends.

It took several minutes before the pandemonium settled enough for all to begin wondering what Pelham voiced first. "But where is Gil?"

Chapter Nine

When it became clear that some mishap had befallen Lord Threlbourne, Pelham mounted his carriage again and wheeled his horses around to retrace their route. Curzon directed his guests back to the mansion, where a general leave-taking began as curricles and carriages left standing during the race quickly filled up with passengers, though none decamped immediately. Noise and confusion reined as high-spirited horseflesh resisted efforts to curb them until Threlbourne's fate had been learned.

Elspeth had not watched the race, but had retreated indoors with Gilbert's mother, Lady Margaret, and Curzon's elderly grandmother. She emerged now, obviously prepared to snub Pelham, but just as obviously on the alert for sight of him. Davida saw her eyes dart over the crowd. When she realized he wasn't there, she approached Davida, who was standing somewhat aside, watching the drive nervously for some sign of her escort.

"What has happened, Miss Gresham? Why is everyone staring down the drive. And you look worried. Has something happened to Mon—to someone?"

Davida heard the alarm behind the carefully modulated question. *So she does care for him, in spite of her behavior,* she thought, relieved for Monty's sake. "I hope not, Lady Elspeth. Pelham has gone to search for Lord Threlbourne. He didn't return to the finish line."

Relief flooded Elspeth's tense features. "I do hope he

is uninjured. This sort of thing is why I cannot like racing."

Lady Margaret, by now aware of her son's failure to return, approached the two young ladies with concern written all over her face. "That madcap boy! If he has hurt himself . . ."

"There they are!" Davida strained to see. "Yes, Monty has Gilbert in his curricle."

In moments the disheveled red-haired lord was jumping down to embrace and comfort his tearful mother. Then he turned to Davida. "Sorry, Davie. My curricle is finished. Came a cropper on a turn and flipped it over."

"Oh, Gil, are you hurt?"

"I'll have a few bruises," he admitted ruefully, "but I'll do."

"And your cattle?"

"Can't be sure, but I think they took no harm. I'll ask Curzon to stable them for a few days."

"And I'll drive you home, Miss Gresham." Curzon had approached the group as they talked.

"I am sure Lady Margaret will take me up."

"But it will be quite crowded in the landau. Besides, it will be an honor and a privilege to drive you." Curzon moved subtly but firmly to block her from joining the group drifting toward the landau.

Although his manner was smoothly cordial, there was something hard about the expression in his eyes which made Davida uneasy. She remembered the black looks he had given her more than once during the day.

Suddenly unwilling to be alone with Curzon, she looked around, seeking some sort of refuge. She realized she was hoping to se Pelham, though she wasn't sure why. But he was nowhere in sight.

"Come, I've had my second favorite pair hitched. They're sweet-goers, too." He turned her toward a curricle just wheeling into view, drawn by a beautiful pair of strawberry roans. The carriage was painted exactly the color of the horses and picked out in cream trim. Davida was distracted by her admiration of this showy rig. She petted the fine animals and talked to them as Curzon waved the last of his guests good-bye. Uneasiness forgotten, she willingly let herself be helped into the vehicle.

Admiration of his team and pleasant reflections on the outing gave them sufficient topic for small talk for the first part of the journey. Then, to her surprise, Curzon suddenly turned off the main road into a country lane just before they entered the outer perimeter of London. He set the brake on the curricle and dropped the reins.

"What are you doing?" Davida turned alarmed eyes upon a suddenly grim-faced escort.

"Don't be frightened, Davie. That's what Pelham calls you, isn't it? I only wish to be private with you a moment."

"Well, I don't wish to be private with you. It is getting dark. My parents will worry."

"This will only take a few moments." His hands suddenly grasped her shoulders firmly and turned her toward him. "I want to talk to you about what happened on the lakeshore this afternoon."

"Lord Pelham said you were put off by that. I am sorry if you are disgusted by the discovery that I have interests other than gowns and balls. I'm not a bluestocking in disguise, if that is what you are thinking. But I do find many things interesting."

Curzon sneered. "I know you ain't a bluestocking, and I have no objections to your intellectual interests. Indeed, a young woman with more hair than wit would bore me senseless."

"Then what?" Mystified, Davida searched the strong, regular features, hardened by intense emotion—barely suppressed anger, she guessed.

"I don't like coming in second, Davida. I would have been very annoyed to have lost the race this afternoon.

But that would be a small matter indeed to being second in my wife's affections."

"I don't know what you are talking about." Davida found Curzon's hands hurtful and struggled to free herself.

"I am talking about your obvious affection for Pelham. Or Monty, as you call him. You *do* call him Monty, don't you Davida, and let him call you Davie, though you insist *I* call you Miss Gresham! No wonder Elspeth is jealous."

Davida was left speechless by this, mouth open but no ready retort coming to mind. Now she understood his ill humor. He was jealous of Pelham.

"In case it has escaped your notice, *Miss* Gresham, I have been courting you in dead earnest, and you have behaved as if you were free to entertain my suit, but you are not, are you?" He gave her a brief, angry shake, his fingers digging into her shoulders.

Davida drew in her breath and bit at her lower lip. Her heart was racing with alarm, but she felt it was time for plain speaking.

"I do like Lord Pelham. He is my friend. Perhaps I might have wished that he would be more to me, but he loves Elspeth very much. I'd be a fool to place my affections there."

"And you are no fool, are you, Davida?" Curzon's lips curled with sarcasm. "But can affections be so wisely withheld or bestowed? Rather, aren't you merely keeping a highly eligible suitor on the string in spite of the fact that you can feel nothing for him."

"Before one's affections are deeply engaged, yes, I believe they can be wisely bestowed—or withheld. In spite of the opinion of many males, we females *are* capable of rational behavior, though I could never marry where I felt no affection." Davida spoke firmly.

"Now let me go and turn these horses around." A long silence followed as her tormentor stared into her eyes as

if he would bare her very soul. At last he drew a deep
breath, and his fingers eased their grip.

"Then bestow your affections on me, pretty sprite.
They will be very wisely bestowed, I promise you." Curzon drew her to him, bending his head to kiss her. She
attempted to turn away, so he trailed kisses along her jaw
line and down her neck.

"Don't," she hissed, turning indignantly. To her surprise, she found she had no wish to be kissed by Harrison Curzon. But he wasn't paying any attention to her
wishes. His hand came up to catch her chin and hold her
still while his lips pressed hers firmly.

Davida froze. She'd never been kissed by a man before, really kissed. If this was kissing, it was most unpleasant. Curzon's mouth had looked full and soft, but
now it felt hard against her lips, and the pressure in-
creased as she resisted him, as if by force he would
make her respond. She tasted blood as her lips were
ground against her teeth.

She whimpered with the pain and he drew back. "Forgive me, Davie. It's just that you excite me so." His en-
circling arm was a steel band, and he lowered his other
hand to mold her breast, pressing her tender flesh boldly.
His eyes glittered with an emotion Davida had never
seen before, but which she strongly suspected was lust.
She remembered Pelham's warning and began to be
truly frightened.

This was the underlying truth behind all the propri-
eties she'd been taught and had observed out of obedi-
ence and a wish for acceptance: men were dangerous!
The isolation of her situation terrified her. She looked
around her wildly, but saw only high hedges on either
side of a deserted lane.

Her eyes flashed with fear and she began to struggle
violently. Surprised, Curzon loosened his hold. Pushing
him away, she choked back a sob to demand, "Take me
home!"

Curzon tried to soothe her. "You needn't be alarmed, Davida. I'm not going to ravish you." He reached out to draw her near him again. She panicked and slid out of the seat of the curricle.

"Devil take it, I didn't mean to frighten you. Come back here. Look, I'll turn the horses as soon as you settle in your seat." He tried to grab her by the wrists, but by twisting them violently she managed to slide eel-like entirely out of the carriage.

The second her feet hit the ground Davida was running. She ran toward the London road as if demons were following her. But she couldn't keep up the pace very long. Gasping for breath, she slowed to a walk, but kept on going, not daring to look around.

Harrison Curzon sat in his curricle completely discomposed. He'd obviously frightened Davida Gresham out of her wits, which was certainly not what he'd intended. Perhaps he had been a little rough with his lovemaking, but he'd never had any complaints before. Still, she was a complete innocent. He ran a hand through his blond curls distractedly. Now what was he to do? He truly cared for the little brunette, who now looked as though she were determined to walk back to London.

He pulled up beside her with his curricle. Davida knew she couldn't outrun him, but she kept on walking as fast as her feet would take her.

"Davida Gresham, do you mean to walk to London?"

She made no reply. With a sigh, Curzon again braked his team and climbed down to run after her. At this she did begin to run again, but he caught up with her quickly and spun her around. The look in her eyes made him back off.

"Davida, I won't molest you again. I swear it. I just got carried away. You can't walk back to London, you know. Now get in the carriage and let me take you home before your parents have spasms."

Davida stood trembling, listening to him and observing his expression. He seemed honesty contrite. It was true enough that she couldn't walk all the way to London.

"Swear on your honor you'll not touch me again."

"Only to assist you into the carriage."

Davida eyed him measuringly for a long while and then hesitantly returned to her seat, trembling all over. True to his word, Curzon immediately gave the restive horses a flick of his whip. He set a spanking pace, glancing at his passenger's set white face from time to time.

"Davida, hasn't your mother explained anything to you? I became aroused by your beauty, your nearness. It is a man's nature."

She turned her face away with a half-stifled sob.

"You know my intentions are honorable. I want you to be my wife. In fact, I'll offer for you this very evening. Please look at me, Davida, and say you forgive me."

Her mouth throbbed where his lips had pressed hers against her teeth, her shoulders ached where he had grasped her, and her wrists felt bruised where his fingers had circled them. Add to that the indignity of that intimate caress—how dare he touch her there! Far from forgiving him, she wished him to perdition, but feared to say so. Having learned that men were dangerous, she was careful to avoid doing or saying anything to provoke him. She kept her head averted from him, fighting back the tears but saying nothing.

He didn't speak again. The drive home was silent. Curzon's expression mirrored his grim realization that he'd given her a disgust of him. In the gathering darkness he put all of his energies into tooling the curricle as nimbly as possible through city streets from which the light was rapidly fading. When they reached Davida's home it was all but dark.

Before Curzon could come around to assist her, Davida was already out of the curricle. He caught her halfway up the steps. "I'll come in and speak to your father now."

"No." Davida turned and faced him squarely, her usually merry face stern. "There's no need."

"There's every need."

"I'd rather you wouldn't. We will not suit."

"Davida, please."

"And I never gave you permission to use my first name, *Mr.* Curzon." With that Davida turned and ran toward the waiting footman. He held the door; within, Perry's round face showed concern. "Miss Davida. Your parents are that worried!"

"Where are they, Perry?"

"In the drawing room, miss."

Davida raced into the room and into her mother's enfolding arms. Unknown to her, Curzon had followed her. She heard her father angrily confronting him. "What is the meaning of this, sir?"

"If I could speak with you alone, Sir Charles, I would like to explain." Curzon towered over her father, but his manner was that of a supplicant.

Davida's father looked from the tall blond man to his sobbing child, and he scowled darkly. "Perhaps you had best return tomorrow to do your explaining. I would like to talk to my daughter just now."

Curzon turned toward Davida and Lady Gresham, his hand held out in silent pleading, but found no ally there. Indeed, the look Davida's mother shot him would have frozen a statue. He dropped his hand and turned away. "Perhaps that would be best. But I *will* be here tomorrow. I would like to have your word that you'll hear me out, sir."

"You have it," Sir Charles snapped. "Now if you will excuse us."

He watched Curzon exit, and then approached his wife and sobbing daughter. How sweet was the comfort of his arms to Davida. The tears came quickly and both

parents patted her and soothed her until the first storm
was over. When at last she could speak, she lifted her
eyes and looked at her father sadly. "Oh, Papa. I've just
whistled down a fortune. I hope you are not angry with
me."

"Angry with you? I'll call that young puppy out for
this! What did he do to you?" Quickly Davida sketched
the afternoon's events for her parents.

Her mother turned Davida's face to the light. "Look at
your poor bruised mouth. That brute!"

"Are you sure he did no more than kiss you? You may
tell me everything, Davida." Her father's voice was omi-
nous in its calm.

"Truly, Father, that is all."

"I'll break his aristocratic nose. Calls himself a gentleman."

"He said he would offer for me, but I don't want him
to." Davida felt it necessary to soothe her father's wrath
for his own safety's sake. She wanted no duel to result
from this day's mishaps. "He only kissed me once, but I
didn't like it, not at all. You won't make me marry him,
will you?"

"Certainly not. He's obviously not the man for you."
Striving for a lighter note, her father added, "Just as
well. He has no title, and I do fancy calling you 'my
lady.'"

"Oh, Papa." Davida sighed against her father's chest
as he patted her back. "I'm afraid I'm going to be an
ape-leader. There was no one I liked better than Harrison
Curzon. I really thought I'd found my husband."

"Tch. You like young Pelham well enough."

"He doesn't count, though. He's going to m-m-m-
marry Elspeth. He l-l-loves her." She jumped up and ran
from the room.

"I thought that was the way the wind blew," her father
observed.

"Much good it will do her," her mother sighed. "I'll go up to her."

"He ain't shackled yet."

"Oh, Charles, do face facts." Lady Elizabeth stalked from the room, her frustration clear in her set face.

"I am," Sir Charles muttered as the door closed behind her. "And fact is, whether she knows it, or wants it, our daughter is head over heels for Lord Pelham."

Chapter Ten

Davida kept to her room for three days after the picnic. She was indisposed, her callers were told, and it was true. She'd caught a mild cold, and was content to lie abed drinking hot possets and reading, in a desultory fashion, the latest of Mrs. Radcliffe's novels. That she also had some bruises and a swollen, sore mouth, none needed to know.

Not even her father knew the extent to which she'd been bruised in her struggle to escape from Harrison Curzon's curricle. Her mother had agreed to keep silent from the same fear that Davida had—that Sir Charles would assume much worse behavior on Curzon's part than had actually occurred, and insist upon a duel or a marriage.

Almost equally bruised by the frightening incident was Davida's usually resilient and optimistic spirit. She felt she would never want to trust herself alone with a man again, and that her search for a husband had ended once and for all, in dismal failure.

In spite of her insistence that he not do so, Harrison Curzon called on Sir Charles the morning after the picnic to ask for Davida's hand in marriage. He was firmly denied permission to pay his addresses. His attempts to get around Davida's father by appealing to his more sophisticated knowledge of a man's passions met with no success.

"Rushed your fences, my boy," Sir Charles growled.

"And rough handling, too. Some women like it, I suppose, but most don't. Certainly not the thing for my Davida."

Curzon looked down, his mouth tight. "I know it, sir. Do you think I have any chance of recovering?"

"I doubt it, and I don't mind saying I hope not. My Davida is a spirited gel, but sensitive. Don't think you're right for her. Her mother didn't think so from the first. Women sometimes seem to know these things.

"Fact is, I think you'd regret it if you married her. You want a different sort of a female, I think."

Curzon shook his head. "I want her. But truth to tell, I've half a notion she favors someone else. In which case, I'm well out of it."

Sir Charles did not pretend ignorance. He laid a finger aside his nose. "As to that, she doesn't really understand her own mind, I'm guessing, and better that way, since that ignorant bantling hasn't the sense to return her feelings."

"Yes," Curzon mused. "He seems set on Elspeth, who'll bear-lead him and make him miserable."

Unable to reconcile himself to failure, Curzon tried again. "Will you permit me to call on Davida, to attempt at least to regain her friendship?"

Sir Charles had his own reasons for agreeing. An abrupt and obvious coldness between the two would lead to talk, and it would be best to avoid becoming scandal broth if at all possible. "I shall speak to her. She was quite shocked by your behavior, though. You must give me your word of honor that you'll make no attempt to be private with her without my express knowledge and permission."

"Agreed."

They parted on reasonably cordial terms. Sir Charles waited until the next day to discuss with Davida her future relationship with Curzon. He and her mother agreed that outward friendliness was required to prevent talk.

"Papa, I can't. It makes my knees quake just to think of being near him."

"Now, Davida, you are not such a milk-and-water miss. I am not asking you to allow the man to court you, merely to be polite to him. Do you want all the tabbies speculating on why you disappeared for several days after the picnic and then would not speak to your former suitor?"

Slowly Davida came around. "I suppose it would not be at all the thing. But I won't dance with him."

"I doubt he'll ask, but if he does, you mustn't refuse, unless it is a waltz. That I'll not ask of you." Her father's stern voice made Davida turn to her mother for assistance. But Lady Elizabeth was entirely in agreement with her husband. "It would be very noticeable if you were to refuse to dance with him. But I think, Charles, you might attend the first ball or two with us, to keep an eye on things. If he does ask her to waltz . . ."

"I shall call him aside and put the idea out of his head. Now what do you say, Davida?"

"I . . . I shall try, Papa."

As she lay in her room nursing her cold and her bruises, Davida cast her mind ahead to the remaining month or so of the season without enthusiasm. Even if any new suitors turned up at this late date, she was terrified of the possible results of a hasty courtship. And the possibility of having to dance with Harrison Curzon made her extremely uneasy.

Her father praised Sir Ralph Moreston to her more than once, but she only stared at him unencouragingly. It had suddenly become clear to Davida something of what the physical intimacy of marriage could mean, and she was quite definite that she would not marry Sir Ralph. The very thought of him kissing her was enough to turn her stomach.

She filled some of her time with addressing invitations to her and Sarah's joint come-out ball, which was

just three weeks away. She also made out place cards for
the dinner to be held beforehand. The duke had placed
one very special and surprising name on the guest list:
the Prince Regent. "A duke has a certain noblesse
oblige, too, you know," he had drawled at the girls when
informing them that His Royal Highness must be invited.

Neither Davida nor Sarah were at all sure they wanted
him to attend. Both were rather intimidated by the
thought. As Davida stilled her trembling hand to address
his invitation, she consoled herself with the unlikelihood
of Prinny's acceptance. She knew he had been ill quite a
bit lately.

Of course, if it were known that the Prince Regent
was coming, their ball would be just the complete
squeeze that was fashionable. But even this thought
didn't cheer Davida, for she felt that she had met all of
the eligible men already, and none of them seemed to be
likely suitors. Besides, they had set the ball very late in
the season—far too late to begin any new courtship, it
seemed to Davida.

"Perhaps I'll just be an old maid," she told Sarah fret-
fully. Sarah had been admitted to her room three days
after the picnic with an admonition from Lady Elizabeth
to coax her daughter out of her megrims. Sarah had been
told a somewhat edited version of the truth, and Davida
was careful to wear a long-sleeve wrapper that hid her
fading bruises. It was not that she feared Sarah would
gossip. She just wasn't up to telling her all of the details.
It would be like living it all over again.

"Silly goose," Sarah laughed. "You don't mean that. I
know! You can marry my father. He promised he'd offer
for you if you came back unattached." The two girls,
sprawled on Davida's large bed, giggled over this teasing remark the duke had made while Davida and Sarah
were showing him some of their new gowns. Then Sarah

rolled over on her back and stared up at the canopy. "He looks at you so, I sometimes wonder if he's just teasing."

"Sarah!"

"I mean it. Would you mind so much?"

"Well, I warn you, I would be a most strict and repressive stepmama!"

Giggles shook them again, and then it was Davida's turn to be serious. "Your father is handsome and kind, and not really so terribly old. He is all of twenty years younger than mine."

"True. He married the day of his majority, and I was born nine months later."

Both girls laughed, half embarrassed by their half knowledge of how this might have come about.

"So he's not quite forty, Davie. It's not an unheard-of difference."

"No," Davida drawled uncertainly. "But I don't love him. I like him, but . . ."

"Oh, I'm sure my father is too old for *love,* though. I mean, isn't he?"

The two girls looked at one another in perplexity. "Then why would he want to marry?" Davida puzzled over this.

"For companionship, I suppose. He knows I'll marry soon. As soon as Gregory comes up to scratch." Sarah's round face took on a militant mien. Her heart had been set on marrying her second cousin and nearby neighbor, Gregory Allensby, since she was fourteen, and this diffident youth seemed devoted to her, too, but as yet had not declared himself. Sarah had hoped he would propose to prevent her going off for a season, but he hadn't. And at any rate her father would not have let her accept until she had had a season in London. She was biding her time until they returned home.

"I suppose your father will be lonely, a little. But you won't live far away if you marry Gregory."

"If!" Sarah protested.

Davida laughed. "But truly, Sarah, I'm not at all certain I want to marry, anymore, and besides, I'm sure the
duke was just teasing me. Though it's so hard to tell
what he means, he has such an ironical way of speaking."

"I almost wish he wasn't teasing," Sarah mused. "If
you married my father . . ."

"And you married Greg . . ."

"We'd always be together," they both finished, laughing.

"Anyway, Davie, do get up and go for a drive with
me. You barely have a sniffle now, and I'm dying to look
at the latest fashions."

They spent a pleasant afternoon shopping, and Davida
felt ready to emerge from her self-imposed exile, so the
family went to the opera that evening to hear Herr
Mozart's exquisite *Magic Flute*. She was reasonably certain not to encounter Mr. Curzon, who had confessed
that he cared little for the opera.

Davida dressed with her usual care, even though she
had the discouraging feeling that it didn't really matter.
She wore a pale plum-colored satin gown with a high
waist and low neckline. The small bruises Curzon's fingers had left on her shoulders were covered by a long,
soft shawl around her shoulders. Her long gloves covered the faded marks where she had twisted her wrists
free of his grasp to escape his carriage.

Her maid had swept her hair up off her forehead with
a pearl circlet, displaying the widow's peak which Mrs.
Burrell had attributed to her Ancaster lineage. Her
pearls went very well with this dress. In spite of her
megrims, she felt returning self-confidence as she in-
tercepted admiring looks while they made their way to
their seats.

During intermission their box was agreeably filled
with young men, including Gilbert Threlbourne. "Lord

Threlbourne," Davida greeted him gaily, "I see you have survived your curricle wreck. How are you?"

"Don't 'lord, me' Davida Gresham. It is all your fault my curricle is smashed and my cattle knocked up."

"My fault?" Davida felt a little twinge of guilt, but looked as innocent as she could, batting her eyes theatrically.

"Yes, baggage. If Curzon hadn't been in such a pelter to impress you . . ."

"No fair," Davida protested, blushing and wishing the subject hadn't come up.

"He drove like a madman. Ran me right off the road. But I see the fair maiden was unimpressed." Gilbert winked at her.

Now what did he mean by that? Had word of her refusal already gotten out? Davida wondered. "Oh, I was vastly impressed that three young men would make such sapskulls of themselves."

"Now who's being unfair! No, it's your fault, and so, you must go driving with me tomorrow in my new curricle and admire my new team excessively."

Davida agreed, glad for the friendship of this likeable red-haired, freckled-faced peer. Ever since he had told her of his understanding with his cousin, she had been relieved to know that he wasn't making any push to engage her affections. His family had long sought the marriage to his cousin for dynastic reasons, but Gilbert was pleased with their choice. He had told Davida, laughing, "She has as many freckles as I have, and hair just as carroty, so we shall suit very well."

It was a new and welcome experience to have a man who was just a friend, and at this point in her life she felt that she needed all the friends she could obtain.

"Oh, I say, Pelham won't like that at all." Gilbert looked over Davida's head to a box directly across from theirs. Davida turned to see Lady Elspeth entering on the arm of Viscount Whitham.

"Then Monty and Elspeth are still quarreling? I had hoped they would have made it up by now."

"Don't know. They've both been playing least in sight since the picnic, but it looks as though Monty is still in the suds with Elspeth, don't it? She'd best be careful. She'll push him too far one day."

The bell for the next act interrupted, and Gilbert bowed to her and left with the others. Davida tried to listen to the music, but found it difficult as she observed Elspeth and Whitham. There was something very possessive about his manner toward her tonight, and Elspeth was looking particularly smug. Davida was trying to feel unhappy for Monty's sake, but not entirely succeeding.

The next morning Davida went down to breakfast just as her father was finishing. He had a peculiar look on his face, almost triumphant, as he tossed the *Morning Post* to her. "Item in the announcements you may find interesting," was all he would say as he kissed her on the cheek and exited, but she could swear she heard him chuckle as he strode from the room.

It didn't take her long to find that Lord and Lady Howard were "pleased to announce the betrothal of their daughter, Lady Elspeth Howard, to Donald Endicott, Viscount Whitham."

Davida felt her heart pounding heavily in her chest. *Poor Monty,* she thought, fighting down the feeling of elation that was trying to break free. She knew his heart would be broken. As his friend, she should be truly sorry, but she very much began to fear that Curzon had the right of it. She had strong feelings for Lord Pelham, and now she could admit they were more than just friendship. *Besides,* she justified her thoughts, *I don't really think they'd suit. She doesn't seem to appreciate him as she ought.*

She allowed herself a daydream of a time, perhaps in a year or two, when Pelham might have recovered from his disappointment. Perhaps he would begin to see Davida as something more than a friend, and court her in form. How delicious that would be.

But her more sensible side told her that it was all a hum. Elspeth's behavior at the picnic, when she had thought Pelham injured, had revealed a deep caring. Doubtless she would repent of this engagement and cry off so that she could marry Monty.

"Davida, wherever are your wits? I've said good morning twice, now."

Davida turned with a start to look at her mother standing in the door to the morning room, where the family preferred to breakfast informally.

When Davida made no answer, but just looked at her uncertainly, Lady Elizabeth sat down and took up the paper. "Your father said for me to read . . . oh, here it is."

Davida watched her mother read and reread the announcement, two small frown lines appearing between her eyebrows. Finally she set the paper down and looked into her daughter's bright blue eyes. Just now those eyes were brimming with tears. For as she watched her mother, Davida realized how many avid eyes were devouring that same news item over breakfast.

"Oh, how could she do it to him? All over the city the *ton* is reading that. Everywhere he goes people will be staring at him, wondering how he is taking it. Why couldn't she be kind enough to wait until the season was over?"

"Perhaps it was meant to be cruel. The poor young man."

"Mother, you mustn't let father throw me at his head. He has some sort of notion . . ."

"Yes, I know, dear."

"But I believe this is only a temporary start. And even if it is not, Monty needs time. Do you think we could go home as soon as our ball is over? The season is almost at an end."

"You may be right. It won't be easy to convince your father, but I'll talk to him."

It would certainly have been most difficult to convince her father that Lord Pelham needed time to get over Elspeth before Davida could find a place in his affections. For that young man was just now closeted with Sir Charles in the library.

Chapter Eleven

While Davida was nursing her cold and her bruised spirits, Pelham was coming to grips with his problems with Elspeth. When he returned home the night of the picnic, his mother noted his grim face and tense demeanor immediately.

"May I take it from your Friday face that all was not well at the picnic?" Lady Pelham was close to her son and felt no hesitation in inviting him to share his problems with her.

On a long, tearing sigh, Pelham threw himself into an overstuffed chair opposite her in their comfortable book-lined library. He dangled his legs over one arm and rested his head against the back. "Ah, Mother, I begin to wonder if I have made a serious mistake." He told her of Elspeth's waspish, stuffy behavior at the picnic. "Even if I could coax her around, do I want to, I wonder? Perhaps we are not suited."

A careful silence ensured, and Pelham straightened in his chair. "Mother?"

"Are you asking for advice, dear, or just for a listening ear?"

"Advice, I suppose. Though"—he flashed her his impish grin—"I don't promise to take it."

"In that case I shall feel much freer about giving it. Courtship is often very stressful. It may be that Elspeth and you would pull in harness together very well in spite of these spats. However . . ."

"However?"

"It may be that your natures are too dissimilar. You must consider carefully what you know of her nature, setting aside her beautiful and socially accomplished exterior, and what you know of your own."

Pelham nodded, dropping his head into his hands. "I have been doing just that all the way home, and what I am beginning to believe—well, I have already told you."

"I hope you will take into account what you need from marriage. If I do not mistake you, it is not just someone to provide you with an heir, but someone who will be a loving partner to you. Coldness and conflict in your marriage will not be as tolerable to you as they are to some other men."

"You and Father set the pattern for me, you know."

"Yes, I know." She smiled warmly in remembrance. "Compared to many women, I was truly blessed in my husband. And the woman you marry will be truly blessed in you, if she only has the wisdom to realize it."

"You've carefully avoided directly giving me your opinion of my marrying Elspeth."

"I don't think I should. I think general principles can be applied . . ."

He grinned at her and moved to kneel in front of her, tenderly taking her crippled hands in his. "You don't fool me for a minute, you know. How long have you felt she was wrong for me?"

Lady Pelham chuckled. "An interfering mother can become very unpopular with her grown children. But to tell the truth, I began to wonder when I heard the *on dits* after your recent visit to Vauxhall. You know there is very little that escapes the prying eyes of the *ton*."

Straightening and flushing deeply, Pelham began to pace the room. "Didn't know you'd heard about it."

"I heard that she had slapped you hard enough to leave the print of her hand on your face."

"Ah!" Pelham rubbed his jaw in rueful reminiscence.

"I doubt you are the sort to make untoward advances. Is it merely my mother's pride that tells me you were not terribly forward?"

"I stole a kiss, that is all. And a gentle kiss at that."

His mother let out her breath slowly. "How glad I am she cried off. You are free, now." At the pain on his face she shook her head. "Not entirely free—it will be a time before you can get over her, for I am persuaded you felt strongly about her."

"That I did. Do. It is very hard to give her up, even knowing that it is the wisest thing to do."

"Do nothing, for a few days, I beg you. This may not be the right decision. They say that love conquers all. Do you think Lady Elspeth loves you?"

"I think that her feelings are somewhat like mine— she loves me but doesn't like me very well."

"I am not at all sure how to deal with that kind of relationship. Your father was ever my best friend."

"Yes, I remember. It seems to me something very precious, something that eludes me completely with Elspeth."

Lady Pelham stood and stroked his cheek tenderly before taking his arm. "Do you dine with me this evening? I believe it is almost time."

During the course of their mostly silent meal Pelham turned over and over in his mind the events of the day and the conversation with his mother. As the last cover was removed and the sweetmeats placed before them, he suddenly burst out, "But hang it all, whom shall I marry?"

Eyes twinkling, Lady Pelham rose to leave him to his port. "That, too, I suggest you do nothing about for a while. Perhaps next year . . ."

He shook his head. "I really wanted to marry this year. The . . . the succession, you know." The fact was that Pelham was a grown man with needs that weren't being met. His conscience wouldn't let him play the rake, and thus marriage had become an urgent priority with him. There were some things you just couldn't say to a mother, though, however understanding she was.

"But I can't think of anyone else right now I would want to marry, except . . ."

"Except?"

"Perhaps I ought to court Miss Gresham. She is a delightful girl." Pelham groaned. "Who is probably accepting an offer from Harrison Curzon even as we speak. If ever there was a buck truly caught in the parson's mousetrap, it is he. He looked daggers at me each time I spoke to her. And I think she means to have him if he asks her."

"Well," Lady Pelham offered as she left the room, "Davida is a very sweet girl, but if she has given her heart elsewhere, I do not think you would want her even if Curzon doesn't offer for her."

"She cares for him, certainly, but I do not think her affections are seriously engaged. Still, that father of hers is pressuring her to marry well, and Curzon's fortune must weigh heavily."

"Such considerations often do. Truly, Monty, I think you had best give yourself some time." Lady Pelham closed the door and left her son to mumble over his port.

Pelham buried himself in neglected correspondence and estate business the next two days, deliberately keeping himself too busy to think of Elspeth. By the third evening after the picnic he was quite tired of duty and domesticity, and sallied forth to Brook's to see who was abroad. He was in no mood for Tories tonight, even if White's was the place he'd most likely find Lord Carrothers, whose dry wit and trenchant observations he would have valued greatly.

His search for lively company was successful. He found several friends at the faro table observing Harrison Curzon, among others, betting heavily. On catching sight of him, Curzon waved Pelham over. "Join us, Monty. I'm in luck tonight. Gonna break the bank."

Pelham was a little surprised to find Curzon well-to-go, his speech slightly slurred and his stance unsteady. Harrison could drink like a fish and never show the least sign of being drunk, a capacity which Pelham had envied him on more than one occasion.

"You know I don't bet against the house, Harry. One always loses in the end. Whist's my game."

Somewhat truculently, Curzon snapped, "Never lose. Don't lose anything. Do I, Oscar? Peter?" He applied to others in the group, who cheerfully called out various insults.

"Nope, never lose. Except at love. Come, then, Monty. A game of whist." He walked a little unsteadily toward a card table, drawing with him two other players.

Pelham sat down with misgivings. He was stone-cold sober, and the other three had obviously been drinking heavily. It seemed a bit unfair, but they insisted. "You'll soon catch up. Have a brandy."

That was too true to deny. Pelham was as well known for his limited capacity for strong drink as he was for his skill as a whipster and marksman.

Several hours of deep play ensued, with sums moving back and forth across the table with no clear advantage. It seemed to Pelham that Curzon had some need to prove himself against him. There was an undercurrent of anger running through all his conversation. When at last Pelham stood up, swaying slightly, and threw down his cards, Harrison had won a tidy sum from him. "I'm out," Pelham announced.

"Whatsamatter, Elspeth jerking your chain? What will she say when she learns you've been a bad boy again?"

Pelham looked down at Harrison, whose usually clear blue eyes were somewhat out of focus. "It's nothing to do with Elspeth. I'm a great believer in the Golden Mean, and I've given you as much *gold* as I *mean* to."

The others chuckled, and Curzon stood up. "Beat you again. Beat you in the race, beat you at cards. Damn you, the only prize I've lost to you is one you don't even want."

Pelham met Curzon's glare, but shrugged his shoulders. "Don't know what you're on about, but I think for once you're as foxed as I am. Let's call it a night."

"Call it what you like. I'm invincible." Curzon shoved his chair back impatiently and headed for the faro tables again.

Pelham turned a puzzled face to the other two players, Arnold Lanscombe and Sir Oscar Rhodes. "What's up with Harry tonight? Never saw him so out of curl before."

Lanscombe drawled insinuatingly, "Could have something to do with the fact that Miss Davida Gresham has shut herself in her room and sees no one."

"She has a cold, that's all," protested Sir Oscar.

"That is what her parents put about. But I saw her in his curricle quite late one evening, looking very disheveled and upset. And everyone thought Harry was on the point of offering for her, but have *you* seen any announcement?"

Pelham straightened up. Usually alcohol made him sleepy or silly, but his drowsiness was suddenly burned away in a surge of pure fury. He recalled Stanley's question: "Afraid Curzon will give your protégé a slip on the shoulder?"

He stormed over to Curzon, grabbing him by one arm and spinning him around. "Damn you, if you've injured Miss Gresham in any way, I'll call you out!"

Curzon, too, suddenly seemed sober. Eyes narrowed, he drew himself up, his six-inch advantage on Pelham emphasized. He shrugged his shoulder free of the strong restraining hand and looked furiously at the other two men, who had followed Pelham from the card table.

"Who says I've hurt Miss Gresham?"

"Talk is that her 'cold' was caught by staying out too late and going a bit too far with London's celebrated 'Golden Rake.' Some say she is ruined but refuses to marry you, and her parents have locked her up until she agrees. Some say you want her for a mistress and her family is preventing her from coming to you. Some . . ." Lanscombe seemed either too drunk or too caught up in spreading his malicious gossip to sense his danger.

Curzon pushed past Pelham and lifted Lanscombe by his shirtfront, suspending him one-handed in midair. He wrapped his other hand around the dandy's formerly exquisite mathematical cravat, tightening it ominously.

"If Miss Gresham's parents say she has a cold, she has a cold, and that is all. She is a pure, proper, and entirely innocent young lady, and I'll have the gizzard of anyone who spreads anything to the contrary!"

Lanscombe had turned pale. He choked out past his taut cravat, "C-c-certainly won't hear it from me. I've nothing but the g-g-greatest respect for Miss Gresham."

"Don't forget. If one word to the contrary gets back to me, you'll know my steel!"

Curzon dropped him as if he were a dirty rag, and turned back to Pelham. "Good to know Miss Gresham has a champion in you, Monty, but in this case, there's no need. She's taken no harm from me. Rather the reverse." He looked down at his feet for a moment and then continued. "Offered for her and she turned me down. I haven't given up yet, though. Once you and Elspeth are leg-shackled, I'll renew my suit."

He gave Pelham a hard, assessing look and then shrugged his shoulders angrily. "Poor sot, to prefer a bear-leader like Elspeth Howard to Davida Gresham."

Sudden silence brought to Curzon's attention the fact that all eyes in the room were riveted on him. Throwing up his arms and laughing, he challenged, "What's the matter? Hasn't anyone else ever been disappointed in love? Drinks for everyone on me, and then gather round. Mean to break the bank."

As the group surged around the tall blond, Pelham turned away. His fury had abated at Curzon's defense of Davida, but Harry's words gave rise to interesting speculations. *It sounded as if he believed Davida refused him because of a* tendre *for me,* Pelham thought.

Wide awake and feeling quite sober, the young baron decided to walk home. As he strolled the few blocks, he mulled matters over. *Could* Davida have a *tendre* for him? At their last meeting she had seemed to be contemplating marriage to Curzon. Yet she had hardly been heartbroken by the thought of having alienated her wealthy suitor.

On the other hand, she had never given any hint of feelings for himself other than friendship. Well, there was that evening when he escorted her to Almack's. His mouth turned up a little at the memory of her startled reaction when he had kissed her hand. Still, mere awareness of him as a man didn't qualify as a *tendre*. And at every turn she had willingly abetted him in winning Elspeth back, hardly the behavior of a woman in love.

No, if Davida had refused Curzon, it was for some other reason. Perhaps they had quarreled over her interest in fossils? But Curzon didn't seem the type who wanted an empty-headed ninnyhammer. And as for his sharing Elspeth's theological qualms, the mere idea was laughable.

The tale of Davida being seen with Curzon, disheveled and upset, bothered Pelham. The thought of it made him curl his hands into fists and wish he had Harrison in front of him so he could plant him a facer. Though probably exaggerated, this story sounded of a piece with what he knew of Curzon's amatory style. If he'd tried anything rough with Davida, that was probably why she'd refused him. She seemed the sort of girl who would hate being man-handled.

Curzon was likely looking for a reason to blame someone else for her refusal. As Pelham climbed the steps to his family's mansion, he concluded that Davida didn't have a *tendre* for him. But as she had turned down Curzon, she was free. They liked each other—that friendship that his parents had so treasured was already blossoming between them. She could perhaps learn to love him, if he played his cards right.

She'd make an admirable wife. Stanley had said so, and as Pelham let his thoughts drift over Davida's person and manner, he agreed. She was good-natured, attractive, intelligent, and socially adept, if a bit beneath his touch. But he cared nothing for that. If he could win her affection, he felt she would be a loving wife, and that weighed heavily with Pelham. Yes, by God, he'd court her!

Undressing without waking his valet, Pelham began to lay his plans. He would escort her during the remainder of the season, as often as could be. Threlbourne lived not too far from the Greshams. He'd wangle an invitation there during the summer, so he could visit her. Then he would invite Sir Charles and his family to the Pelham country seat for the hunt. A cosy house party would be just the place to fix his interest with Davida.

If only this wretched season were over. There was entirely too much time left for his comfort. Sir Charles might yet find another suitor for his daughter.

But it wouldn't be seemly to offer for her himself so soon after breaking off with Elspeth. That would be like a public insult to his former fiancée, and he still cared enough for her not to give her pain.

Have to drop the old man a hint, Pelham thought, *to prevent his pressuring her into marriage elsewhere.* In the wee hours of the morning Pelham fell asleep while happily making plans for a leisurely courtship of Davida Gresham. He knew he'd have to go slowly. For one thing, she might think less of him if she thought his feelings for Elspeth had been shallow. For another, she might think he was merely turning to her on the rebound.

And that wasn't true. Oh, no, not in the least. Curzon was right. Elspeth was a bear-leader. Delectable, but a bear-leader, nevertheless. Pelham firmly suppressed the vision of Elspeth in all her blond loveliness that rose to taunt him, and turned his mind to tallying the charms of his future fiancée.

When his valet answered his ring with his morning chocolate and the *Post,* Pelham saved the announcements until last, not expecting to see anything of interest to himself there.

Suddenly he exploded, hitting his tray with the paper so savagely that chocolate flew everywhere.

"Damn and blast," he yelled, leaping from the bed and tossing his astonished valet his chocolate-soaked robe. "Send me a footman to order my curricle, and then lay out my clothes at once. That hussy thinks she's breaking my heart, sure as I'm born. Well, she'll catch cold at this game."

As Pelham stormed about the room, his curious valet glanced at the paper and saw, at the head of the announcements, the news of Lady Elspeth's engagement.

A scant hour later, Montgomery Villars, Baron Pelham, awaited with outward calm and inward trepidation the arrival of his soon-to-be fiancée. For though Davida would be astonished by this sudden proposal, she liked him, and dutiful daughter that she was, she certainly wouldn't go against her delighted father just because she had been caught by surprise.

Would she?

Chapter Twelve

Davida and her mother were startled when Perry interrupted their breakfast to announce in a formal voice, but with an interesting twinkle in his eye, "Miss Davida, Sir Charles requests that you join him in the library as soon as is convenient."

Mystified, Davida instantly abandoned her kippered herring and followed Perry to the library, entering as he opened the door. She was astonished to find Lord Pelham and her father standing near the fireplace, talking amiably. Her father was obviously very pleased.

"Here she is now. Come here, Davida. As you see, we have a visitor."

Forcing herself to be calm and not betray her newly acknowledged feelings for him, Davida curtsied and held out her hand. "Oh, Monty, I was so sorry to hear . . ."

"Ahem." Her father cleared his throat loudly. "I'll just leave you young people alone for a few minutes."

Davida turned startled eyes to Pelham, who had an enigmatic look on his face.

The closing of the library door seemed as loud as a shot in the preternatural silence as Pelham and Davida faced one another.

Suddenly Davida burst out, "Ohhhh, Monty, you great looby. Tell me you haven't offered for me!"

It was Pelham's turn to be startled. "But I have. Why should I not?" Then he had the grace to look a little sheepish.

"That is carrying our strategy entirely too far. Father thinks you are in earnest. He wants us to make a match of it. He'll never let me cry off, at least not without a great to-do, and . . ."

"Why should you cry off, Davie?"

"Because you want to marry Elspeth. Don't pretend not to understand me."

He drew himself up, a dark scowl on his face. "Elspeth is marrying Whitham and good riddance to her."

"You don't really mean that! If she were to cry off, to come back to you, of course you'd want to marry her."

"No, I wouldn't. She's played her tricks off on me once too often. I want a comfortable wife, one with some fun and spirit in her, not a starchy puritanical . . ." He was beginning to pace, spluttering with fury.

"Don't you see? Your very anger says how much you still care for her! Oh, Monty, I could just kill you for this. My father will be so upset. But you must go to him at once and explain."

"No need for him to be upset." He thrust his hand through his dark auburn curls, disarranging them entirely. "Mean to marry you. You'll have me, won't you, Davie?" He moved swiftly to seize her by both elbows, pulling her near.

"Say you will. You know we'll deal well together."

"Deal well? Is that all you want from marriage? Just to 'deal well' with your wife?" Davida was becoming furious. She jerked out of his hands. "It's not enough for me! Selfish looby. Didn't you give any thought to *me* in this? Don't you think you should have found out what *my* feelings were before you approached my father? What if they're engaged elsewhere?"

"Are they, Davie?"

"Perhaps they are!"

Pelham's face took on a determined look. "*Are* your affections engaged? Who could it be? Not Curzon. I saw him in Brooks's last night, Davie. He was very well to go, wrapping himself around buckets of the best French brandy and muttering about rushing his fences. He told me you'd refused him. He's the only one I ever thought had a real chance with you."

"Perhaps it was just a lovers' quarrel. Perhaps I only wanted a little time to think."

"He seemed to believe it was a fairly firm refusal. He seemed to blame it on your feelings for . . ."

"Bother what he thought." Davida's cheeks flushed. This turn of conversation had to be avoided at all cost. "Monty, you are just upset by Elspeth's engagement. Why don't you wait awhile. In all likelihood she'll change her mind. Live a carefree bachelor's existence until you know for sure. Why the rush into the parson's mousetrap?"

"Don't want her even if she does change her mind, and I don't like a bachelor's existence. I've know for some time that marriage was the right path for me." Pelham caught her up again and began drawing her, gently but inexorably, toward him.

"I want my own soft woman in my bed at night."

Heart racing, Davida felt the strangest tremor rush through her as Pelham drew her into his arms and enfolded her there. She felt nothing of the fear or discomposure that had overwhelmed her when Curzon had held her thus. Her head tilted back as he bent ever closer. "But, Monty, are you saying just any woman will do? Because . . ."

His kiss silenced her. How different from Curzon's hard pressure. Gentle, coaxing, stirring, his mouth moved over hers. Davida sighed and leaned into him, returning the pressure of his lips instinctively. They stood thus for long, entrancing moments, exploring one another's lips in delicious detail.

At last Pelham lifted his head. "No, not just any woman will do, Davie. But *you* will do very well."

Davida recognized in the almost black intentness of

his cobalt blue eyes an emotion very akin to the lust she'd seen in Curzon's a few days before. But it didn't frighten her. Not from Pelham. Instead, it accelerated her breathing and led her to eagerly match his ardor when he returned for another long kiss.

How wonderful it felt to be in his strong arms! A strange fire sang through her body, and her knees felt weak, so that when Pelham at last came up for air, she clung to him helplessly, her head burrowed in the curve of his throat.

Completely focused on each other, the young couple had not heard the click of the latch as the library door opened. Her father's hearty voice made them both jump. "Well, well, I see it's all settled, then!"

Davida came to her senses and tried to struggle free of Pelham. "No, Papa, it isn't. We, I, that is, he . . ." she stammered.

Pelham gave her no help. Instead, tucking her firmly against his side with one arm, he extended the other to Sir Charles. "Indeed it is, sir. You may wish us happy."

"Excellent." Sir Charles turned and called to Perry. "Fetch us some champagne and send Lady Elizabeth to wait on us in the library."

"Monty, you will regret this when Elspeth changes her mind! Help me stop it before it goes too far." Davida's pleas only made Pelham shake his head, an amused look quirking his mouth.

"What are you saying, missy?" Sir Charles's voice was rough with indignation.

"Oh, Papa, don't you see? Lord Pelham has proposed to me in a fit of pique because of what Lady Elspeth has done. He doesn't really want to marry me."

"Yes I do."

"And I don't want to marry him." Davida managed to pull away and move toward her father, hands held out in supplication.

Sir Charles drew himself up and fixed on her as se-

vere an eye as she had ever known from her usually in-
dulgent parent. "Do you mean to tell me that I walk in
here to find you plastered to this young man, kissing him
like a . . . a . . . and there is no engagement?"

Davida retreated a step, fetching up against Pelham's
firm body. He brought his hands to her shoulders to
steady her.

"What Davida means, sir, is that she has not yet formally accepted my offer. But of course, as you say,
under the circumstances, it is understood."

"I should hope so." Davida felt herself withering
under her father's accusing stare.

"Well, daughter?"

"Yes, Papa." Cheeks burning, she lowered her eyes.

Lady Elizabeth rushed into the room just then, closely
followed by Perry bearing a tray of glasses and champagne.

"Davida? Lord Pelham? What is going on?"

"Oh, Mama!" Davida started toward her mother, hoping to pour out her misgivings and gain an ally, but her
father caught her arm and spun her around.

"Our daughter has just accepted Lord Pelham's proposal of marriage, that is all." There was both pride and
determination in her father's voice, and Davida knew the
game was up. She flashed a furious look at Pelham, who
bowed mockingly to her before stepping forward to accept the glass of champagne proffered by the round-
faced butler.

"A toast to Lord Pelham and his soon-to-be-bride, my
beloved daughter, Davida Gresham. May they be as
happy and as blessed in their marriage as I have been in
mine," her father intoned formally. They all lifted their
glasses and drank the effervescent wine.

Davida's mother still seemed shocked, but a pleased
pink suffused her cheeks as she addressed Pelham. "This
is a surprise, my lord. A very sudden, but delightful surprise."

"Thank you, Lady Elizabeth. I feel truly fortunate to be granted such an adorable bride." He smiled down at Davida, whose head was feeling a little muzzy from the champagne. She looked at him blankly, unable to figure out how to alter the flow of events.

"Shall we plan on a long engagement, my lord?" Lady Elizabeth sounded hopeful.

"Yes," Davida quickly asserted. "A long, long engagement."

"No," Pelham drawled at the same time. "If we have the banns cried at services this Sunday . . ."

"Sunday!" Davida gasped.

"We can be married in, say, four weeks, right at the end of the season. All of our friends will still be in town. So much more convenient for everyone, and I confess I am eager to have my affairs settled."

"I see." Lady Elizabeth frowned a little. "But a wedding requires such a lot of planning. I don't know . . ."

"Stuff and nonsense," Sir Charles growled. "We can plan a perfectly fine wedding in four weeks."

"But, Papa, you are forgetting how busy we are planning for my come-out ball."

"It needn't be a large or elaborate affair, if you prefer," Pelham assured Davida and her mother. "In fact, if you wish, I will see the archbishop about a special license and we can be married very quietly in a few days."

"No," Davida and her mother replied at the same time.

"I can see my daughter wed in fine style and I will do so. We shall contrive, shan't we, my dear." Sir Charles placed his arm gently about his wife's shoulders, but there was a hint of steel in his voice.

Lady Elizabeth capitulated to her husband's determined tone. "Oh, yes, I know we can. And a spring wedding is so lovely."

"Excellent. Now why don't you and Davida go off and begin planning, while Lord Pelham and I discuss settlements?"

Davida and her mother soon found themselves standing in the foyer with the shut library door at their backs.

"Well! I hope that young man of yours knows what he is doing. Your father is extremely pleased by this liaison."

"And he'll *never* let me cry off. Oh, Mother." Davida turned into her parent's comforting arms.

"Let us go upstairs where we can be private, love." Lady Elizabeth gently led her daughter away. "Do you wish to cry off?" she asked as soon as they were safely ensconced in Davida's bedroom. "I think you have a *tendre* for him."

"I do," Davida wailed. "I love him so much it hurts."

"Then why?"

"You know why, Mother."

"Yes, I suppose I do. You are afraid he'll spend his life wanting someone else."

"It's even worse than that. If I thought Elspeth would really marry that chinless wonder she's engaged to, I'd marry Monty without hesitation. I know I'll make him a good wife, and he's too good-natured to fail to respond to that."

"But you think she'll cry off and try to get Pelham back."

"Yes. I expect she was just angry and wanted to punish him. And don't you see . . . If I don't let him go, if Papa insists on the engagement, Pelham will do the honorable thing, but he'll blame me. He will always see me as having stood between him and his beloved. What chance of happiness would we have then?"

"Well, Davida, if it comes to that, I am not without influence with your father. And I've never known him to be cruel."

Her arms were around Davida in a soothing hug, rocking her back and forth as if she were an infant. Davida took comfort from the embrace and her mother's words.

"We'll just have to see what happens, dear. Perhaps

you are mistaken and Lady Elspeth means to wed Lord Whitham. Now dry your eyes. The word has already spread among the servants, I'm sure. We don't want any Gothic rumors of force and unwilling brides to begin to circulate."

"Oh, no! How awful *that* would be. Pelham would completely fail in his plan if Elspeth thought I wasn't willing."

"Surely you don't think this proposal is just a ploy to bring Lady Elspeth around," her mother cried. "Lord Pelham wouldn't be so cruelly selfish, would he?"

"I don't know, Mother, but I know this. I don't think he ever thought of me as anything but a friend until today."

Her mother's eyebrows arched with curiosity.

"When he kissed me, I think he was as surprised as I was at how . . . umm . . . good it felt."

Her mother failed to suppress an amused smile. "Well, there is some hope, if he felt . . . umm . . . *that*."

"Is . . . *that* . . . enough for marriage, Mother?"

"Not really. However, you also like and respect one another. Many successful marriages have been based on no more."

"Your marriage to Papa was a love match, wasn't it?"

"Well, it was on my side, at least."

"On *your* side. Oh, Mother. I don't believe that. Father adores you."

"I know he truly loves me now. But his affections were not deeply engaged when we first wed. It was more a question of ambition. When he returned from the war, newly knighted and with his estates to improve, I feel sure the fact that my grandfather was an earl weighed heavily with him, as did my large dowry. After all, I was too tall, and too shy to attract so dashing a *parti* otherwise.

"I fell madly in love with him. He was so handsome in his soldier's uniform. His name was in all the papers for valor, you know. And he was full of plans to improve farming methods and build up the quality of livestock in this area. Such a sense of purpose was vastly impressive to me.

"When Sarah's father introduced us, I knew my dowry and my breeding figured largely in your father's interest. I didn't care. In fact, I was just glad I had *something* to bring me the husband I wanted.

"So you see, love came later for him. In fact, I am fairly sure exactly when he realized he loved me."

"When was that, Mama?" Davida forgot her own concerns in hearing this unknown story of her parents' relationship.

"When I nearly died giving birth to your older brother."

Davida knew her mother had lost a child four years before she was born. Lady Elizabeth's expression showed that the memory still had the power to cause her pain.

"He was so distraught, so full of fear of losing me. He swore he'd never touch me again in that way, so as never to risk me again. Of course, it was a promise I didn't want him to keep, but I had quite a time persuading him otherwise." Lady Elizabeth looked a little embarrassed at this frank speech, but her daughter was soon to be married. She would need to know something of these things. "How glad I am that I succeeded, else I never would have had you, dearest, or Petey."

"So, you see, love can grow. Don't despair of good coming from this engagement." She gave Davida another warm hug.

"Thank you, Mother. I won't."

But long after her mother left, Davida's mind raced back and forth over the delightful sensations she had experienced when Pelham kissed her, and her fears that Lady Elspeth would change her mind. Rarely had she been in such a quandary, torn between joy and misgivings.

She was quite starved when luncheon was served, and went down to find Pelham seated in the dining room with her father and mother. "Ah, there you are, my dear," her father called. "As you see, we have a guest."

Davida smiled shyly at Pelham and took her place.

"Thought as I'd been here so long already, might as well stay for a bite and then take you for a drive."

"Oh! I can't. I'm promised to Gilbert. For a drive, I mean."

Pelham laughed. "Daresay he'll yield to me on the day of our engagement. We'll look at rings, what?"

"Excellent idea." Her father shot her an admonitory look.

"Very well, Lord Pelham, if *you* will explain to Gil. He was most insistent that I try out his new team."

"Surely we can have done with this Lord Pelham business once and for all now." Pelham laughed. "From now on, I am Monty to you all, and you are Davie, before the whole world."

"Davida, if you please," Lady Elizabeth interjected indignantly. "I have a lovely daughter. I heartily dislike hearing her called by a man's name."

"Ah, yes, she warned me you'd ring a peal over me about that. Davida, then, at least in Mama's hearing." Pelham winked at her in an endearing fashion as he took some slices of thinly shaved ham onto his plate.

Davida felt her heart turn over. How she adored him. How she wished he returned her love in full measure. Instead, she was second best and, she was quite sure, owed her engagement to Pelham's pique at Elspeth's announcement. He would wish to be released from the engagement the minute Lady Elspeth broke off with Lord Whitham.

Chapter Thirteen

Lord Threlbourne stood in front of Davida and Pelham, looking back and forth between them as if believing and hoping one or the other would begin laughing and give the joke away.

"Engaged! You two? Stap me if that ain't outside of enough. Cut line, will you?"

"Don't matter how much cant you bedazzle us with, Gil, the fact remains. Today I have asked Miss Davida Gresham to be my wife and she has accepted me." Pelham's manner as he repeated his announcement was smug.

"It won't do, Monty. It won't do at all. Not good *ton*."

Pelham drew in a sharp breath. He had known there would be some eyebrows raised at his fiancée's obscure family. With his title and fortune, he could have looked very high in the ten thousand for a wife. But he certainly had not expected such a good friend to blatantly object.

"Now see here, Gilbert. Won't have you insulting my intended in that way."

"Not insulting her." Threlbourne turned to Davida and took her hand, patting it fondly. "Davida is good *ton*, right up to her pretty little ears. But you, Pelham. This dashing from engagement to engagement just won't do. You and Elspeth are behaving like children."

Real temper began to show in Pelham's voice. "This has nothing to do with Lady Elspeth. I haven't been dashing from engagement to engagement. And I won't

let you put a damper on our happiness." He glanced
rather anxiously at Davida, who had grown progressively more agitated as this conversation continued.

"Happiness!" Davida tossed her head with a most unladylike snort. "He is only saying what everyone else
will say. I tried to . . ."

Pelham quickly interrupted her. "Yes, I know, dear,
you tried to get me to postpone our announcement for a
while, but I can't wait to make you mine. Get your
pelisse and we'll go shopping for rings." He gave her a
not very gentle nudge toward the door. "Sorry to deprive
you of her company today, Gil, but I know you'll understand."

"Oh, I understand, well enough," Threlbourne intoned
gloomily, trailing them down the steps.

Once he had her settled in the curricle beside him,
Pelham began a rapid-fire monologue that deliberately
gave Davida no opportunity for further discussion.

"Of course, I could give you a family heirloom.
Mother is still wearing her ring and wouldn't part with
it, but it wouldn't suit you anyway. None of our old
pieces will, the rings, at least. You have your own style.
I picture you with something light. Perhaps a star sapphire set in diamonds. Your eyes aren't quite sapphire,
though."

He caught and held her eyes with his deep cobalt
gaze. "Lovely eyes, bright blue with flecks of white and
amber like little lights in them. First thing that I really
noticed about you, Davida, was your sparkling eyes.
And don't shoot fire at me with them now, missy. It
don't become you!'

"Spanish coin, sir," she began, but he leaned over and
stopped her protest with a quick, firm kiss on the mouth,
then laughed gleefully at her discomposure.

"Mother will be so pleased. She thinks highly of you,
you know. We'll call on her later this afternoon and tell
her the news."

Davida clearly recalled his mother's rapture when she thought there was a rapprochement between Pelham and Elspeth. "No, Monty, I must insist you tell her alone. It isn't fair to her. She hopes you'll marry Elspeth. This will come as a shock to her."

Pelham knew his mother would be surprised and somewhat disapproving of this sudden engagement, not because she wanted him to marry Elspeth, but because she had urged him to give himself time to be sure what he wanted. She would be most censorious of his precipitate action in proposing to Davida. So he dropped the subject of visiting his mother that day.

"Let's agree not ever to mention a certain young lady's name between us. It will lead to a much more harmonious relationship." He lifted her hand, turned it over, and kissed it warmly at the wrist, just above her short gloves. Davida drew in her breath, feeling a tingling begin at her wrist and spread through her like lightning. He knew just how to get around her, she thought, tugging indignantly on her hand.

He refused to relinquish it, however, but held it in his own as he drove. She allowed herself the luxury of enjoying his touch, quite forgetting that three days before she had been wondering if she could ever endure any man's touch.

By the time the fashionable hour for driving in the park had arrived, Davida was possessed of a lovely sapphire ring just as Pelham had described. As they greeted acquaintances, her newly acquired fiancé saw that the news of their engagement began to spread. Soon they could not move two paces in the park before being stopped by someone wanting to know if it was true.

Her ring was admired and Pelham congratulated until Davida thought she would cry, for she felt sure that most of those smiles and expressions of delight were thinly disguised sneers of derision at this hasty engagement. She felt sure all recognized it for what it was, a reaction

to Pelham's being jilted. Indeed, more than one supposed well-wisher alluded to the coincidence of their becoming engaged on the same day as Lady Elspeth and
Viscount Whitham's announcement.

Pelham seemed unaware of any such undercurrents,
but after a time he realized that she was miserable. "Are
you getting the headache?" he asked, looking at her with
concern as she frowned and bit at her trembling lip. Trying hard not to let him see the tears beginning to gather
in her eyes, Davida nodded.

Her distress bothered him, and he searched for words
to relieve it. "I'll take you home and you can rest for a
while. You'll want to be fresh for the Talbots' ball
tonight. What a pleasure it will be to escort my beautiful
fiancée there."

Davida turned her head aside. "I mean it, Davie. I'm
very proud of you. I'm looking forward to showing you
off."

"I . . . we weren't invited to the Talbots' ball. We were
to attend a musicale tonight. In fact, I am to sing."

"In that case, we'll go to the musicale. I've been
wanting to hear you sing."

"Have you really, Monty?" Davida searched his face
hopefully.

His expression was warm, almost tender. "Yes, Davie,
I have. Very much. I've been told you have a lovely
voice. When we are wed, I will have my very own opera
singer!"

Tears threatened to overwhelm her, and he turned his
horses toward the gates, picking up the pace to prevent
further interactions with the fashionable *monde*.

After the musicale, Lord Pelham sat with his friend
and mentor, Stanley, Lord Carrothers, cracking a bottle
at White's.

"She sings like an angel. And she's pretty as she can
stare. Good-natured and affectionate . . ."

"Then I may take it you are happy with your choice," drawled Lord Carrothers.

"Very. No self-righteous posings for my Davida. Not that she isn't a good girl. She is all that is proper. But not starchy and supercilious like—like some I could name."

"Are you trying to convince me or yourself?"

"Hang it all, Stanley, you sound like her. I'm convinced she's the best choice for me. Don't you think so?"

"I never interfere in affairs of the heart, dear boy."

"Well, this isn't exactly an affair of the heart. Mean to say, I've made a rational choice for a change. Not that I don't care for her." His lips curved in a reminiscent smile. "You should have seen how she melted against me when I kissed her. She's a bewitching armful. And I am beginning to believe Curzon may have had the right of it when he hinted she had a *tendre* for me."

"Rational choice, eh? Yes, I can see that!" Carrothers chuckled.

"Rational choice doesn't rule out affection," Pelham snapped.

"No, of course it don't. In fact, I agree with you, rationally speaking. Mean to say, Elspeth is the fashionable beauty, of course, blondes being all the crack. But you have the right of it. Her looks won't hold up like Davida's, that's for sure. And in all points relating to temperament Davida is clearly superior."

"Not that I care a pin, but how can you doubt Elspeth will remain a beauty? Her features are quite classical, like a miniature bit of Greek statuary come to life." Pelham felt himself oddly inclined to be insulted by this slight to his former fiancée.

Adopting a professorial tone, Stanley lectured, "True, but compare the mothers. Now if a man wishes to make a *rational* choice"—Stanley gave the word 'rational' an ironic twist—"he will pay less attention to the daughters, and more to the mothers."

In his mind's eye, Pelham pictured Lady Howard and shuddered. She was a forbidding-looking woman, short and very round, with three chins and a basilisk stare.

"Quite so!" Stanley gave his pupil a quick grin. "Lady Elizabeth is matronly, to be sure, but very nicely proportioned, and with a very pleasant demeanor."

"And only one chin!"

"You begin to understand me. I have to admit, now that you are well out of it, I have been worried for you a bit, my boy. Lady Howard's personality has quite a chilling effect on one, and Elspeth bids fair to be just like her."

Pelham was much stricken by this observation. It was good to have Stanley's support, for he was painfully aware that his fiancée and his mother, to say nothing of many members of the *ton,* felt he had engaged himself to her entirely in retaliation for Elspeth's engagement announcement. To have his good friend applaud his actions was a longed-for balm.

"Then I am, as my mother said, well out of it, on yet another ground." Somewhat morosely he drew the brandy bottle to him and poured another drink.

"Dipping deep, tonight, Monty. If you are so pleased with your choice, where is the worm in the apple?"

"There's no worm. None at all!" Pelham's denial was truculent.

"You still love Elspeth."

"No, hang it, I don't. That harpy has quite killed any feelings I had for her."

"Then what?"

"Let go, Stanley."

"If you wish it. But you are down-pin about something, and I'm ready to listen."

"You know me too well." Pelham dropped his head into his hands. "Davida thinks I only proposed to her because of Elspeth's engagement."

"Which is not true." Stanley quirked an inquisitive eyebrow.

"No, damn it. As I said, I was planning to move in that direction anyway, though by means of a carefully planned courtship. When I heard that she'd turned Curzon down, I was very relieved. Especially after he as good as told me he thought she had a *tendre* for me."

"But you rushed your fences, eh?"

Pelham lifted his head and met his friend's sympathetic brown-eyed gaze. "Yes. I jumped in and proposed when I heard about Elspeth's engagement, without preparing the ground. I had it in mind to court her, to win her, but now she thinks it's all to spite Elspeth. It's hurting her, and I hate that."

"Unfortunately, most of the *ton* thinks the same."

"That's part of what is upsetting her. But it's not true. Not at all. Except for the timing, I mean. So what's to do?"

Stanley shook his head. "It's not a game I play well, or I suppose I wouldn't still be a bachelor."

"I'll make it up to her. S'all I can do. Take her everywhere, let her see I don't care a snap for Elspeth."

"And if you find out that's not true? If she changes her mind and wants you back, can you honestly say you won't want her?"

"Hang it all, I won't. But even if I did, I wouldn't hurt Davida by crying off. Never cry off, no matter what!"

Stanley's mouth curved in an ironic smile. "Yes, that should certainly make Davida happy, to marry her but prefer Elspeth."

Pelham brought an angry fist down on the table. "Told you! I'm well over Elpeths . . . Elspeth." He stood up, aware that he had consumed too much brandy. "Can't make even you believe me, can I? Much less Davida. Going home." He stumbled slightly as he made for the door.

"Methinks he doth protest too much," Stanley intoned grimly, watching his friend's unsteady departure.

The next Sunday found Davida, her parents, Pelham, his mother, Sarah, and Sarah's aunt, in St. George's Cathedral listening to the banns for the approaching marriage. Davida tried to imagine the reception the banns would receive in their home parishes, where they were also being read this morning. Would Pelham's neighbors be astonished and derisive at his sudden change of fiancées? Would Sarah's father, the Duke of Harwood, feel the slightest twinge of regret?

After many tears and considerable soul-searching Davida had decided to make the best of it, to pretend all was perfect and hope with all her heart that pretense would become reality. So she put away her misgivings and looked up at Pelham with a brilliant smile that caused him to draw in his breath with awe.

She really is a splendid girl, he thought, taking her hand.

He's so dear to me. I hope I can make him happy, Davida thought, letting her hand rest confidingly in his.

Chapter Fourteen

"They make a handsome couple, don't they?"
Lady Elspeth Howard turned reluctantly to find Harrison Curzon standing at her side watching with her as Lord Pelham and his new fiancée, Miss Davida Gresham, completed the receiving line gauntlet at the Fitzwilliams' ball.

Elspeth pasted a determined smile on her face. "Indeed! Charming. So glad Monty found someone to suit."

"And where is your current fiancé, Lady Elspeth? Not retired to the card room with his gambling cronies already, has he?"

Elspeth bristled. "Certainly not! Donald does not gamble! He and several other young Tories are in the library discussing how to pass tougher corn laws, if you must know."

"Ah, a worthy cause, grinding down the poor! Well, at least Whit's *politics* suit you better than Monty's." Curzon's grin was insinuating.

"Oh! Odious man. Everything about him suits me better!"

"But of course. I was forgetting. 'Twas you jilted Pelham."

"Twice, in effect." Elspeth raised her chin proudly. "I ought to thank that scheming little minx. She meant to have him all along, you know. Chasing after you was just a tactic."

Curzon looked thoughtful. "What makes you say that?"

"She caused our quarrel at Almack's didn't she? And at the picnic. Twice she threw herself at him. You were there."

"Yes, I was there, Elspeth, and that won't fadge. Davida could hardly have planted a trilobite on the grounds of Elmwood, nor have foreseen that you would make such a cake of yourself once it was found."

The blonde sniffed disdainfully. "She started that racing madness, though. You can't deny that."

"Actually, I started it, as I recall."

"Well, she urged you on."

"I believe it was more with an eye to being entertained than upsetting you. No, Lady Elspeth, I must speak plainly. Your own self-righteousness pushed Pelham away from you, just as my foolish impulsiveness pushed Davida away from me."

They watched gloomily as Pelham led Davida onto the floor for a waltz that was just beginning. Completely forgetting that she had denied all interest in him a few minutes ago, Elspeth muttered through clenched teeth, "Well, she can't have him, the conniving little witch. Oh! Don't let us stand here gawking like this. Dance with me, Harry."

Obediently Curzon swept her onto the floor, though they were an awkward pair, she so petite, he so tall.

"You still care for him, then," Curzon ventured once they'd entered the rhythm of the dance.

"Yes, and I know he loves me, too. It's obvious, isn't it, that he just got himself engaged to her in retaliation for my engagement to Whit."

"You may be right. How came you to do so cork-brained a thing, anyway?"

"My parents were urging me to forget Monty, since he upsets me so, and praising Whit to the sky. I had some vague notion that it would punish Monty. It would shock

him so much that he'd come and apologize and say he'd
never make me unhappy again and then I'd forgive him.
But now he's engaged to her and everything is so complicated, and . . . and I'm sorry."

"No one is sorrier than I at your momentary weak-
ness."

For the first time Elspeth really looked at Curzon.
"You truly care for her?" A crafty look came over her.
"What did you mean when you said you'd driven her
away?"

"Never mind. It's too late now."

"No, it's not too late. He loves me, and I'm going to
get him back."

"How?"

"I don't know. Perhaps you could help me."

Curzon studied her critically for a few minutes. "You
are a willful, selfish baggage, but if you could succeed in
breaking up that engagement, I would be eternally grateful.

They circled the floor a few minutes without talking
as Elspeth plotted.

"I know! You could compromise her."

"No! I don't want an unwilling wife. What folly! And
you'd regret it if you trapped Monty with such a trick,
too."

"Well, I must do something!"

"I have an idea. I think you are right that Monty offered for her out of spite, or out of a prideful wish not to
appear to have been spurned. I am very much afraid that
something I said to him gave him the idea."

Elspeth turned the looked of an avenging fury on him.
"You! Why?"

"Not intentionally. I was a bit cast-away. Told him I'd
court Davida again once he was safely leg-shackled to
you. Had no idea what you were up to, did I? Anyway, if
we're right, and he does still love you, then you must go

to him and apologize. Tell him why you did what you did, and beg him to forgive you."

Elspeth quivered indignantly. "I can't do that!"

"You can if you want him badly enough."

After another long, thoughtful silence, she began hesitantly, "With your money, you could hire someone else to compromise her, or abduct her or something. You could rescue her, and then she'd be willing . . ."

"Absolutely not! I don't want a wife whose name has been sullied any more than I want one who is unwilling. Listen to me, you virago. If you manage to besmirch Davida Gresham's name or harm her in any way, I'll see that you are paid back in the same coin."

Elspeth shuddered at the intense look on Curzon's face. "Don't get in such a pelter. Oh, all right. I will do as you ask. But what good will convincing Monty do? He is honor-bound to marry her now, and she'll never let him go."

"I'm betting that she will. I doubt Davida would hold on to an unwilling man."

Hope dawned in Elspeth's eyes. "Then help me maneuver Monty into dancing a waltz with me, and I will begin the campaign."

Curzon's features relaxed. "That's more like it. I'll find out when the next waltz is to be played and . . ."

While the two conspirators plotted, Lord Pelham and his fiancée looked to be thoroughly enjoying their waltz together.

A period of activity more intense than anything Davida had ever known before had commenced with her betrothal to Lord Pelham. Every morning she and her mother were up early, hard at work on the myriad details necessary for a wedding, from invitations, to gown fittings, to catering arrangements. All of this was in addition to the ongoing preparations for her and Sarah's come-out ball.

Early mornings they paid or received calls, and their callers were many once the engagement was placed in the papers. When weather permitted, Pelham took her for a drive every afternoon. On the several rainy days during that period, he planned some sort of indoor recreation for them. They visited the British Museum yet again, Lord Threlbourne accompanying them, to see the Elgin Marbles. Of course they attended Madame Tussaud's wax collection, which was in London for the season.

One bitter-sweet outing resulted when Monty had the brilliant idea of viewing the Royal Academy's exhibition of paintings again. Davida noted Curzon's three splendid paintings with a feeling of sadness, but said nothing to her escort about her experience there with Curzon.

Davida's favorite outings were to see the private fossil collections of several members of the Royal Society who were friends of Pelham.

In short, he had been a most attentive fiancé. They selected together their evening's activities, whether it be a ball, opera, musicale, or route, or sometimes all three!

Gilbert complained loudly after the first week, "Never see you in White's or at Gentleman Jackson's anymore. Can't get near Davie to take her driving. D'you mean to live in her pockets all the time?"

"If she'll let me. I rather like it," Pelham had responded, lifting a questioning eyebrow at Davida.

"I like it, too, but you know I don't require it."

"No, that's one reason I like it." He had given her that wicked wink that never failed to cause her heart to flutter.

They had encountered Elspeth and her new fiancé at Almack's the Wednesday after the banns were first cried. The two couples were excessively civil. The men exchanged handshakes and congratulations. The women admired one another's rings and discussed wedding dresses.

That ritual observed, they had since carefully avoided one another, though present at many different events. This evening's ball at the Fitzwilliams' seemed no different. Yet beneath the surface there were undercurrents. Davida was painfully aware whenever Elspeth was present. On this particular evening she had seen the looks the blonde cast their way at times, and correctly interpreted them. She was quite sure that Elspeth regretted giving up Pelham.

This was the first dance at which Curzon had been present since their fateful drive home from the picnic, and she was uneasily aware of him, too.

As for Lord Pelham, he was more aware of Davida's uneasiness than its cause. He had taken note of Elspeth and Curzon, but saw no reason why either should disturb his and Davida's enjoyment of the evening. He was prepared to do the polite and otherwise ignore them.

He was somewhat surprised when Curzon and Elspeth approached them quite pointedly later in the evening. He was not pleased when Elspeth suggested they waltz together for old times' sake, but she asked if Davida would mind in such an insinuating tone that there was nothing for either of them to do but acquiesce.

Pelham was unaware of the full extent of Davida's aversion to Curzon, however. She stood half in shock as the handsome giant held out his hand, obviously expecting her to dance with him. Her father had not seen any necessity to accompany them with Lord Pelham as their escort, and her mother was nowhere to be seen.

"I . . . um. If you don't mind, Mr. Curzon, I'd rather not . . ."

"Shall we promenade, then?"

"No, I . . ."

"Then let us sit with the chaperons. Surely you know I can't ravish you there."

Davida sensed the underlying anger beneath his bantering tone, but agreed to sit with him, not knowing what else to do. They watched the swirling couples in silence for a few moments.

"He's going to break your heart, you know."

Davida turned with a gasp to see the ice blue eyes trained on Monty as he danced with Elspeth. She followed his line of vision and stiffened. "They dance very well together," she responded primly.

"His proposal was prompted by Elspeth's engagement."

"I am aware of that."

"Are you aware that he hadn't a notion of doing so until I inadvertently let it slip that you had a *tendre* for him?"

Davida lifted her chin. "I suspected as much. This conversation is unwelcome to me, Mrs. Curzon."

"I don't doubt it, but not half so unwelcome as an unhappy, leg-shackled husband is going to be. Don't do it, Davida. Give me another chance." He had taken her wrist in a fierce grasp.

"You forget—I would say yourself, but this seems to *be* yourself—you forget where you are!" She stared pointedly at his strong hand.

Immediately he loosened his hold with a groan. "Forgive me. I do seem to forget my self around you. I love you, Davida Gresham. Can Montgomery Villars say the same?"

Tears came to Davida's eyes; she turned her head away.

"I thought not. Let me . . ."

"How I feel about him, or he feels about me, has nothing to say to what I feel for you." Davida's anger overcame her tears. She spoke sotto voce, for the people around them were beginning to stare, but her determination showed in her eyes. "I do not love you, I cannot love you, Harrison Curzon.

"At one time I thought I might. I liked you, and I thought I might learn to love you. But I now know that liking and loving are entirely different. I would appreciate it if you would not embarrass me like this again, or I will not even be able to say that I like you."

Curzon stared away, out onto the dance floor, or into infinity, for what seemed an eternity. Then he rose rather wearily from his seat and gave her a formal bow. "Then it would seem that I am *de trop*. Good evening to you, Miss Gresham."

She watched pensively as he made his way around the ballroom and out the door, then swung her glance back around to where Elspeth and Monty were just ending their waltz. They were laughing together like the best of friends.

"He'll break your heart," Curzon had said. The way it made her feel to see those two so obviously enjoying one another's company, Davida recognized the very real danger that his prophecy could come true.

She was saved from having to confront Monty and Elspeth immediately by the for-once fortunate appearance of Sir Ralph Moreston, who presented himself as her partner for the next dance, a cotillion. By the time she was reunited with Pelham, she had herself well in hand. She said nothing to him about his dance with Elspeth, and he did not bring it up. But the unseen tension was there, and both felt it. When Monty drew her back as her mother left the carriage, hoping for a good-night kiss, he wasn't too surprised that Davida turned her head, offering only her cheek.

As he rode home alone, Lord Pelham contemplated Elspeth's behavior tonight in some perplexity. She had been more like the young woman he had originally courted, full of light, pleasantly flirtatious chatter. She was lovely as usual, and her grace as they danced together could not be denied.

He was pleased that she had decided to hold out the hand of friendship to him, as it would make their life in the *ton* more agreeable. It was a pity that Davida felt so threatened by Elspeth, for while he still recognized his former fiancée as a supremely attractive female, he no longer felt any inclination to make her his wife.

As he mounted the steps to his home, however, honesty compelled him to admit that the case might have been quite otherwise if Elspeth had continued to behave as agreeably as she had this evening. He permitted himself a moment of doubt. Had he been hasty in giving up on Elspeth? Then he slammed the door on that avenue of thinking firmly. Too late now.

Chapter Fifteen

The outing to Vauxhall was not one to which either Davida or Pelham looked forward, though for very different reasons. Davida had been to Vauxhall only once, with her parents, Sarah, and Sarah's aunt. She had found it a disappointment.

Pelham dreaded going because it would remind him of the unhappy night when he had kissed Elspeth on one of the infamous darkened paths of the pleasure garden. Her slap had shaken his own love to its foundation and caused him to question whether she loved him at all.

Making it even less appealing for either of them was the fact that this Vauxhall party invitation had originally been extended when he and Elspeth were thought of as a couple. The occasion was the celebration of the eighteenth birthday of Elizabeth Montmorency, a close friend of Elspeth's, so she would surely be there. Since the Montmorencys were longtime friends of his, Pelham still felt obligated to go.

Unspoken between Davida and him lay the question of his feelings for Elspeth, so he dreaded an outing which would necessarily throw the three of them into company. But even less did he wish to appear without Davida, when Elspeth would surely be escorted by Whitham. He hated the thought of her flaunting her fiancé when his was nowhere in sight.

When he invited Davida, she let her lack of enthusiasm show. "I will go, if you feel we must, but I have to confess it is not my favorite place," she responded when he asked her about her lackluster response. "I do not know the Montmorencys, and I have to confess I did not much care for Vauxhall the one time I have been. It was dull and I got very chilled. These fashionable muslin dresses are not made for the night air."

"I understand, though I am sorry you feel that way. I must attend or risk offending some very old friends. Of course, you may stay at home. A night's rest will do you good." He cupped her chin in one hand and tried to smile encouragingly.

His reluctance to do without her company was obvious in his face, and Davida felt enormously relieved. She had half feared he would grasp eagerly at an opportunity to be around Elspeth without her. She quickly relented. "I expect it will be much more interesting with a party of young people."

"I will insist on your wearing a warm cloak, fashion be damned. Excuse me, but I get quite irritated over such things as adhering to fashion when it makes one ill. For instance, cosmetics with lead or arsenic in them. These young ladies who whiten their faces with blanc—and some of the dandies do the same to their hands—so foolish."

"You won't be ashamed of my unfashionable appearance?"

"By no means. In fact, this would be a good time to wear those infamous pantaloons." He winked at her.

Davida was mortified. He'd never mentioned the offending undergarments before. At her pink cheeks and averted eyes he couldn't resist a quick, tender kiss. "No need to look so abashed, Davida. I've always thought pantaloons an imminently sensible solution to some problems of the female wardrobe."

Seeing that her embarrassment was only increasing, he hastened to change the subject. "And Elizabeth's father has arranged with the Vauxhall management to have special fireworks in her honor. Should be quite spectacular."

"In that case I shall certainly go. I love fireworks." Davida's spirits lifted immediately. "When we visited the gardens, Papa made us leave just as they were starting. It was a re-creation of some battle or other, and I think it brought back very unpleasant memories for him."

On that evening, Davida was glad she had worn a warm cloak, and a very fine, lightweight woolen chemise, though she hadn't quite dared the pantaloons. It had been a mild May day, but as she had feared, the night air was cool and there was a breeze on the water as they approached the park.

She quickly found that attending Vauxhall with a group of young people that included a handsome young man whom she adored was an entirely different experience from attending with her parents and Sarah's aunt.

The fairy lights spread everywhere seemed romantic, as did the music wafting on the night air. She gave Pelham a delighted smile when he asked her if she was enjoying herself. They had arrived early in order to see the Cascade at nine. Davida had not seen this famous fountain on her first visit.

She was fascinated by the elaborate cascade of water that flowed over the mountain scene. Afterward, Pelham managed to divert her briefly down a side path, where he stole a kiss that was most satisfactory to both, before escorting her to the boxes, where he introduced her to their host and wished Elizabeth a happy birthday.

As they talked with the family and guests, Pelham stood close behind her, closer than propriety allowed, and subtly tipped her off balance so that she rested against him. She was embarrassed yet felt a delightful flush run through her whole body. She should have moved away, but she doubted that anyone would remark their closeness in the packed throng of people, so she surreptitiously enjoyed the feel of his strong body against hers.

Of a sudden she felt him stiffen and from the corner of her eye saw his head turn slightly, neck rigid and jaw working. She pulled away from him and turned to follow his gaze. At the edge of the crowd was Elspeth, dancing with her fiancé, Viscount Whitham. Elspeth was wearing a gauzy white confection of a gown, low-necked and high-waisted, and as she wove about among the dancers an occasional shaft of light penetrated the thin gown to reveal that she had virtually nothing on underneath. Her charms were on display for all to see, and Pelham seemed to be taking full advantage of the occasion.

Angrily Davida turned away from him and, finding Claude Montmorency, Elizabeth's older brother, standing nearby, she began to talk to him. Lord Eberlin was a homely but likeable man of around thirty-five, a widower with two children. Davida set herself to entertain him, finding this was easily done if she kept the conversation to horses.

When Pelham tore his eyes from Elspeth, he found Davida strolling arm in arm with Lord Eberlin, drifting away from the group. He quickly strode after them. "Making off with my fiancée, Eberlin?" he inquired in what he hoped was an amused voice.

"Oh, it's you, Monty. Didn't know your gel was a horsewoman. Has a mare that is a descendent of the Godolphin Arabian. Like to see her. Why did you not bring her to town, Miss Gresham?"

Davida firmly retained her hold on Eberlin's arm and smiled up at him, ignoring Pelham. "I wanted to very much, my lord, but she foaled in February and the colt was too young to wean or make the trip."

"How did he turn out? His sire was Thespian's Revenge, you say?"

"He's going to be a beauty. He is a bay, like Thespian,

but with white stockings on all four feet. Papa says he has excellent conformation."

"May just call in on your father after the season. Like to see these animals, what?"

Taking Davida's other arm firmly, Pelham stopped her, and thus Eberlin, in their tracks. "I am sure we will be glad to show you the colt. We will be taking him and the mare with us. Her father means to make her a wedding present of them."

"Pity. Well, perhaps I'll call in on you. A decent interval after the wedding, of course."

Pelham bowed formally. "You will be most welcome, Claude, and now if you will excuse us?" He drew Davida away and started down the south walk with her firmly in tow.

Davida went reluctantly, dragging back against his firm grip. She wanted no more stolen kisses with a man who panted so obviously after Elspeth Howard. "We mustn't lose sight of our party, Monty. Our chaperon . . ."

"Hang all chaperons! What are you up to?"

"What do you mean?" Davida's voice was somewhat shrill, and several other strollers turned to stare at the couple.

"I mean, making up to Eberlin that way. I saw you go after him like a dog after a juicy bone."

"I am surprised that you could see me, since your eyes were glued to Lady Elspeth." Davida tossed her head angrily.

Pelham stopped and turned her to face him. "Is that the problem? Just that I looked at Elspeth? But every male in the place was looking at her, in that scanty costume. Might as well be a cyprian, dressing like that!"

"It bothers you greatly, doesn't it?"

"Now see here, Davida. Jealousy is a very destructive emotion. I know, I just felt it when I saw you with Eberlin. Which is what you intended, isn't it?"

"No, I just didn't want to stand there looking like an ape-leader, swathed from head to toe in a warm cloak, while my fiancé ogled . . ."

"What is this, the lovebirds quarreling already?" Davida recognized Curzon's voice immediately, and turned to see him standing nearby, a very lovely, very immodestly dressed young woman on his arm.

Pelham turned, too, and his frown deepened when he saw the girl. "Just a discussion. No concern of yours, Harry."

"Well, now, I rather think it is. After all, I in a sense played Cupid to you two, didn't I? Don't like to think of my handiwork failing." There was a smile on Curzon's lips, but the ice blue eyes glittered dangerously, and Davida backed up against Pelham.

"Run along, Harry, that's a good boy. Your companion there is not fit company for Davida, as you well know."

As if he had forgotten her existence, Curzon turned and surveyed the young woman at his side for a moment. Then he gave her a little push on the shoulder. "Run along, my dove. I'll catch up momentarily." The girl gave Davida a resentful stare before walking away.

Davida's eyes widened with curiosity as well as dismay at this, her first encounter with the "muslin company." She felt a little sorry for the cavalier treatment the young woman was receiving.

Turning back, Curzon bowed to Davida. "Beg your pardon, Miss Gresham. Do you require any assistance? Shall I escort you back to your party?"

Davida, pressed against Pelham's side, could feel him draw in an indignant breath. Before he could get a word out, though, she rushed into speech. "No, no, Mr. Curzon, all is well. Please do not concern yourself . . ."

"You will always concern me, Miss Gresham."

"That will do, Harry." Pelham stepped forward, anger suffusing his features.

"Yes, I suppose it will. For now. I bid you good

evening, Miss Gresham." He bowed again and walked on.

Davida found that she was trembling uncontrollably. Pelham felt it and put his arm around her shoulder, drawing her a little way down a side path, less brightly lit, on which a convenient bench welcomed them.

"Sit down, Davie. Why are you trembling?"

She shook her head. "He looks so . . . so . . . dangerous. I was afraid he'd hurt you."

"Hurt me? Davie, I'm not afraid of Harrison Curzon."

"Perhaps you should be."

"Look at me!" So unfamiliar was such a tone of command from her fiancé that Davida flinched a little as she met the deep blue eyes, now narrowed and as hard as Curzon's ever had been. "I repeat. I am not afraid of Harrison Curzon. I can protect you from him or any other man, nor do I require you to protect me from him!"

Davida felt the strong force emanating from the young man she had thought of as the soul of gentleness. It alarmed her, yet at the same time it made her feel very secure to know that he stood able and determined to protect her.

"What did he do to you, Davie?" Pelham had not discussed with Davida the reason for her breakup with Curzon. Now his curiosity—and his suspicions—were aroused. "If he has molested you in any way, I'll make him pay!"

"Nothing. It's just that he . . . he was not at all happy that I refused his offer. He was very jealous of you, and I think he's capable of violence."

"Most men are, if it comes to that. But you can't live your life fearing Curzon. If ever he bothers you, I will put a stop to it instantly. Nor can you live in fear of Elspeth, for that matter. You still haven't told me why you abandoned me for Eberlin."

"Oh, Monty, give over. I know you still care about her. The minute you spotted her, you quivered and went stiff, like a bird dog on point. And your indignation about her costume is a bit too like that of a jealous lover, frankly."

"She means nothing to me.

Her eyes reproached him for his dishonesty. He looked down for a moment, and then lifted his compelling gaze to hers. "Old habits die hard, I suppose. I was used to concern myself with her welfare, and I cannot think it best for her to display herself so. But it's none of my concern. *You* are, Davie. Are you still trembling out of fear, or are you cold?"

"I . . . I'm feeling chilled." Davida wasn't sure why she was trembling, but she felt much better when he drew her near, chafing her arms through her cloak.

"Should you like to go home now?"

Davida quickly agreed. The magic had gone out of the evening for her. She walked with him along the lighted walkways, seeing nothing of the whirl of humanity around her, seeing only Pelham's eyes riveted to Elspeth.

Chapter Sixteen

If Davida had been disturbed by the encounter with El- speth at Vauxhall, she was almost devastated when, two evenings later, she entered the withdrawing room at the Duke of Ormond's ball to discover Elspeth following right behind her.

"Miss Gresham, may I speak with you?"

"Of course, Lady Elspeth. What may I . . ."

Abruptly Elspeth began to cry bitterly. "Oh, I love him so much. Why did I give him up? Why?"

There was a great deal more in this vein. Davida awk- wardly attempted to comfort the girl. At last the blonde gained control of herself and stepped away, her back to Davida.

"It's me he loves, you know," she murmured.

Davida said nothing. She couldn't assert the contrary. Though Pelham seemed very fond of her and openly ap- preciative of her good qualities, he had certainly never pretended to love her. She felt her heart beating heavily in her breast, a sense of dread weighing her down.

Correctly interpreting her silence, Elspeth turned to Davida, a look of triumph on her face. "He does! He loves *me*! He'd marry me in a moment if we were free!"

"But you aren't, Lady Elspeth. By your own choice, I might add."

"I would break off with Whitham. I know now it was a terrible mistake to become engaged to him. I only did it to punish Monty. But you'll never let him go, and he's far too honorable to break off himself, even though it's me he loves."

Davida drew back in horror. This was what she had most feared. Struggling for self-control, she measured her words carefully.

"I would never hold Monty against his wishes. My parents, my father would cut up rough if I cried off, but you see, I love Monty, too. I want him to be happy. If his happiness truly lies with you, I'll break our engagement somehow, if I have to run away to do it."

Elspeth reached impulsively for Davida's hands and squeezed them. "Oh, thank you, thank you, Miss Gresham. You are the best of friends to us both. He said you were a good-hearted girl." She turned and swirled out of the room, leaving Davida feeling as if she'd been thrown and trampled.

She found her mother and told her she had a headache. "I'll get Monty," her mother said.

"No, let's just go and leave a message for him. He is enjoying himself in the card room. I hate to call him away."

Her mother gave her a strange look. "I don't think he will like that."

"Truly, Mama, I don't want to cling to him too tightly. He may come to chafe at being forever in my pocket, whether he realizes it or not."

So they ordered Monty's carriage, leaving a message with their hostess that they would send it back for Lord Pelham as soon as they reached their destination.

In the carriage Davida told her mother what had happened. Lady Elizabeth protested, "Oh, my dear, she *can't* try to reclaim him now. We are little more than two weeks from the wedding."

"I tried to tell you and Papa how it would be."

"And besides, she will surely find your fiancé unwilling to end your engagement. I am persuaded he is very

fond of you, Davida, and then it is not at all the
thing . . ."

Davida dropped her head back against the squabs.
"Fond, Mother! How can that weigh against a deep at-
tachment? And do you think I can bear to trap him in a
marriage he doesn't want, merely out of propriety?"

"Say nothing to your father, Davida. He will not be at
all easy to deal with. No sense upsetting him unless we
know it is absolutely necessary. You must discuss the
matter with Monty and determine that it is truly what he
wants, first."

Pelham was on their doorstep at ten the next morning.
"I've come to inquire of Davida's health. She left the
ball early last night complaining of the headache," he informed her father, who was still reading the paper over
his breakfast.

"Ah, yes. Davida is lying abed this morning. I think
she is a little pulled by all of this activity. Elizabeth has
gone off already on one of these eternal fittings. Be glad
you're not a female, m'boy. They spend half their lives
buying clothes and the other half changing into and out
of them!"

Pelham grinned his agreement and companionably accepted his future father-in-law's invitation to join him
for coffee. "Then I've got to push off. Know you won't
credit it, but I've got a fitting, too. Blue coat." He
groaned. "Why do weddings have to be in the morning?"

Pelham's first hint of Elspeth's broken engagement
was just as he was leaving the master tailor Weston after
his fitting. Lord Threlbourne and Arnold Lanscombe
called to him from across the street.

"What's to do, Gil?" Pelham asked after he dodged
traffic to join them.

It was Lanscombe who replied. "Town's buzzing.
Lady Elspeth has broken off her engagement with
Whitham." He watched eagerly for some sign of emo-
tion in Pelham.

"So Elspeth is playing off her tricks on Donald, eh? Well, glad it's his problem now and not mine." Whatever was in his mind, Pelham's countenance was perfectly composed and gave away nothing to the gossiping dandy.

"Betting is already going into the books at White's, Monty, that it *is* your problem." Threlbourne's look was accusatory. "Odds on favorite that you'll break off with Davida Gresham and take a run at Gretna with Elspeth or some such."

"Gretna? With Elspeth?" Pelham's astonishment was genuine. "Surely you didn't lay your blunt on that side, Gil."

The red-haired lord shook his head sadly. "Not betting on this one. But the word is, Davida left without your escort last night, just after a tête à tête with Elspeth in Ormond's withdrawing room. The two of you have been joined at the hip since your engagement, so it's not surprising people are wondering."

Fury was Pelham's primary emotion at this moment. "The witch," he exploded. "It would be like her to tell Davida her plans, and worse. I must be going." He turned abruptly and dashed for his curricle, held at the ready for him by his tiger.

At the Greshams' he found confirmation of his fears in Davida's face. Her shadowed eyes looked at him with anxiety as he entered the drawing room. Several people were seated there, callers avid to share the latest *on-dit* with the Greshams, no doubt. With great effort, Pelham forced his expression to be pleasant and relaxed.

The silence that descended when he entered told him all too clearly what was the topic of discussion.

Briskly crossing the room, Pelham took Davida's hand and drew her to her feet under the watchful eyes of her parents and their visitors. "Sorry to rush you away from your guests, dearest," he drawled, kissing her fingertips lovingly. "But we are invited to tea with my mother. I believe she wants to show you the Pelham jewels this afternoon. Had you forgotten?"

The relief in her parents' eyes and the quick murmur around the room told him his strategy was successful, at least with everyone but Davida. She walked ahead of him like a condemned woman to her execution.

It was a cool, misty day, more like March than May, and Pelham had brought his landau, with the top up. He handed Davida inside and took his seat beside her before she could protest the lack of a chaperon.

"I am sure your reputation will survive a three-block drive with your intended," he responded when she became agitated.

"That does not signify just now. Oh, Monty, is it possible you haven't heard?" Davida searched his face anxiously.

"Heard what, Davie? I've heard nothing that concerns you or me." He picked up her hand and drew off her glove.

"Don't Monty. Listen. Lady Elspeth has cried off." She tried to tug her hand away, her voice choked.

"Oh, that. Yes, I'd heard. She's getting to be a regular jilt." He carried her hand to his lips and began to press light kisses on her wrist and palm.

It was wicked of him to tease her so. Indignantly she confronted him. "Don't pretend it's nothing to you, Monty. I know . . ."

"You know nothing if you think I still want Elspeth! I wouldn't have her. She is fickle, in addition to all her other faults."

"Give over!" Davida cried. "If ever there was a time for complete honesty, this is it. You know you want me to cry off so you can marry her, and I will. I won't hold you to your engagement, Monty."

"No, you won't cry off. Now, Davie, listen to me." Pelham spoke vehemently. "If you were to cry off, and I were perfectly free to do so, I wouldn't marry Elspeth

Howard. I decided the day of the picnic that she and I wouldn't suit. I won't pretend it didn't cost me some pain to give her up, but it was the only solution. We are chalk and cheese. I thank goodness that I found out in time."

"Oh, Monty, are you sure?" Davida felt a rising tide of joy within her as she crept into the arms Pelham gently wrapped around her.

"Not only am I sure and certain that Elspeth and I *won't* suit, I am equally as sure that you and I will. My delight with you has grown day by day, Davida Gresham." He tilted her chin up so he could look her squarely in the eyes. "I am literally counting the hours now until you will be my bride."

Davida sighed and raised her head for the kiss he was intent on bestowing. She savored the delicious fiery bubbling sensations that ran through her. "I can hardly wait, either."

Thus delightfully occupied, it was several minutes before the couple became aware that the carriage had stopped outside the Pelhams' town house, an imposing mansion in the most fashionable street in town.

"Do I look disheveled?" Davida tested her hair and patted at her clothes.

"No, though I am afraid you do have a look about you." The mischief was dancing in those cobalt eyes.

"What . . . what sort of look?"

"Oh, the look of a girl who's been thoroughly and expertly kissed." He smiled smugly as he handed her down from the carriage.

Davida gasped, cheeks pink. "I can't face your mother like that!"

"Nonsense. If she's heard this latest *on dit,* nothing is like to reassure her more."

"Reassure? I am persuaded she would far rather have Lady Elspeth for a daughter-in-law."

"You are fair and far out there, my girl. She already

had her doubts, and when Elspeth got herself engaged to Whitham, Mother washed her hands of her."

Though Davida was dubious, Pelham's mother had never been less than completely cordial to her, and it seemed that she bent over backward to be gracious this day. "Perhaps she hasn't heard yet," Davida whispered as she stood frowning at her reflection in a mirror. Pelham was arranging an elaborate collar of diamonds around her neck as his mother sorted through jewelry boxes laid out on a long table in the back drawing room.

"Let's find out. Have you heard the latest, Mama? Lady Elspeth has ended her engagement to Lord Whitham."

"Yes, you wretch, of course. Several tabbies practically broke down my door to tell me this morning. Did she have the town crier spread the news, I wonder? Here, Davida, these emeralds will become you far more. That piece is too heavy. Monty, you must have them remounted for her. I never liked them either."

"Exquisite," Pelham applauded when Davida had donned the ornate gold-wire-and-emerald necklace.

"Yes," his mother agreed. "It's an old piece, but not as heavy as the other. Davida wears it well. My dear, you must wear it for your come-out. Or, no, I collect it will not go with your gown?" At Davida's nod, she suggested, "Then to the Raleighs' ball?"

"Oh, but should I, before we are married?"

"It will be little more than a week away by then. I don't see why not, unless it won't go with your gown. Ah, I knew there were matching earrings." Lady Pelham lifted them triumphantly from the cascade of precious stones before her. "Try them, too."

Feeling truly relaxed and happy for the first time since her betrothal, Davida cuddled next to Pelham in the landau on the way home, the box containing the Pelham emeralds in her lap. She was finally convinced it was she

Pelham wanted to marry, and she felt truly accepted by his mother.

"What a wonderful day," she sighed as she leaned against Pelham's shoulder.

He grinned and put his arm around her, drawing her close and dropping a quick kiss on her lips.

"You look happy, for once."

"I *am* happy. Oh, Monty. I will try to be a good wife. I think we can deal very well together, don't you?"

"I grow more sure of it with each passing day." A surge of tenderness went through Pelham at her radiant face tilted up to him. She was a delight. How lucky he was to have found her.

In this self-congratulatory mood, Pelham took Davida home and then returned to his own to dress for dinner.

That life was not always going to be quite so pleasant he quickly realized when his butler greeted him with a bit of unwelcome news. "There is a . . . ah . . . person, to see you, my lord," Hilton informed him. "She is in the library."

Chapter Seventeen

"A 'person,' Hilton?" Lord Pelham stared at his dignified butler. He was not accustomed to such visitations as were so many other pinks of the *ton*, and he felt somewhat nonplussed.

"Yes, sir. A young lady, it is, veiled. Didn't give her name, but I am sure you'll want to see her, my lord."

It's Elspeth, as Hilton damn well knows, Pelham guessed with a sinking feeling. The wily butler would have been unlikely to put an unknown female in Pelham's favorite retreat. He entered the library reluctantly.

"Close the door," a too-familiar voice commanded, and then the veiled hat was tossed aside to reveal Elspeth, dressed in an almost transparent leaf green muslin that heightened the green of her eyes and displayed her charms blatantly.

"What are you doing here, Lady Elspeth? You must leave at once." His coldly angry voice lashed out at his visitor.

"Don't, Monty. Please, listen to me. You obviously haven't heard." Lady Elspeth held her hands out to him dramatically. "I've broken my engagement to Whitham."

"Of course I've heard," Pelham responded coolly, ignoring the invitation to embrace her. "Is there anybody in England who hasn't?"

"I thought . . . you might be more pleased to see me."

"I am engaged to be married, Elspeth. Your being here is a serious embarrassment."

"But you can break off your engagement. I know that
Miss Gresham will agree. She told me so last night. She
told me she wanted you to be happy. She's a very generous, good-hearted person."

"Yes, she is, and a great deal more than that, and I
haven't the least desire to end my engagement to her.
Moreover, I am furious with you for approaching her.
She was most upset."

Pelham had warily kept a tall-backed sofa between
himself and Elspeth. Upon hearing these discouraging
words, she collapsed in a heap upon it and began weep-
ing inconsolably.

"I've lost you forever. It's all my fault. Oh, I am so
miserable I want to die," she gasped out between sobs.

So affecting was her desperate sobbing that Pelham
came to sit beside her and pat her shoulder ineffectually.
"Don't, Elspeth, please. We shouldn't suit, you know.
All we ever did was quarrel."

"Oh, Monty." She turned toward him, lifting a tear-
stained but very lovely face to his. "Please forgive me. I
know I've been difficult, but surely you still love me.
Can love die so quickly?" She pressed herself against
him, throwing her arms around him and bringing her lips
to his.

"Here, now." He took her arms and tried to push her
away. "Quite some behavior from the miss who
wouldn't even let me kiss her when we were engaged.
Didn't even seem to like it, now I think on it."

"I know I seem cold to you. But I've been brought up
so strictly. I thought it was wrong. I asked my mother,
and she explained about men and the . . . the intimacies
of marriage. You'll have to teach me, to show me how to
make love." Her eyes seemed huge in her lovely face.
"I'll be a willing pupil," she whispered, pressing against
him again.

It was very difficult for Pelham to resist this shapely,
gorgeous creature when she offered herself to him so

openly. He felt the dull throb that was the beginning of desire. How often had he dreamed of sharing passionate kisses with this delectable beauty? When Elspeth put her lips to his again, he gave in to temptation and bent to return the kiss, drawing her fully into his enfolding arms.

Her fervor was overwhelming. She kissed him back, running her hands through his hair and writhing against him. Aroused by her response, he deepened the kiss, thrusting his tongue past her open lips and probing within.

Elspeth gasped and drew back, rigid with shock. "How can you! You did that deliberately to give me a disgust of you." A look of horror on her face, she dealt him a hard slap.

Pelham recoiled, his face flushed except for the imprint of her palm on his cheek. "No, Elspeth, God forgive me. What I did was let passion overcome me for a moment. Men have a tendency to do that when curvaceous young females throw themselves at their heads."

A dull red suffused Elspeth's face. "You cannot mean I'm supposed to *let* you do such a disgusting thing to me? Does *she* let you do that to her? Davida Gresham must be a wanton degenerate to . . ."

Suddenly Davie's trusting face as she had looked up at him full of joy not many minutes before flashed before Pelham's eyes. *What am I doing?* he wondered. *Not only am I betraying her trust, I am about to hand her over to the tabbies.* He was under no illusions as to how Davida's reputation would fare if Elspeth began spreading such notions about. He jumped up.

"No, she doesn't. Miss Gresham hasn't so far forgotten herself as to tempt me into such behavior."

Elspeth gasped indignantly, but he continued without mercy. "She would never present herself alone in a man's library, nor throw herself at him, as you have done with me. Have a care, Elspeth, or you will become scandal broth."

"*Am* I supposed to let you kiss me that way?" Elspeth was truly puzzled.

"No, no more than you were supposed to come here in the first place, Elspeth."

"Then *she* won't let you either, if she is so proper!"

"There is a time and a place for such lovemaking. I am quite confident that when I do kiss Davida passionately, after we are married, she will not be disgusted. She is a loving, warmhearted girl, and you, Elspeth, are cold and shrewish. Now, please leave."

He took her hat and placed it firmly on her head, drawing the veil over her astonished face as she gasped for words. "You can't mean that," she wailed. "You love me. I love you."

"No, Elspeth, I don't love you. If I ever did, which I begin to doubt, it's gone now. And you don't love me. I doubt if you can. You just want me to dance to your tune again. But I never will. If for no other reason, I would not do anything so shabby to Davida Gresham. But there are many other reasons, so give it up."

He finished tying the veil firmly in place and propelled her to the door. "I hope you find happiness, Elspeth, but it can't be with me. Now please go, and do not come back."

After his unexpected visitor departed, Lord Pelham sank into his favorite leather chair and brooded gloomily on the fact that he had so easily fallen prey to Elspeth's charms. *Pray God Davida never knows of this incident,* he thought.

That evening as they arrived at the Malcolms' ball, Davida was happier than she could ever remember being before. Not only was Pelham attentive, but he obviously took pleasure in her company. Feeling the security of knowing he truly wanted to marry her, Davida let her love show. She blossomed into a radiant creature so alive to Pelham's every mood that it seemed to her that he was already the other half of herself. Even though he had never spoken of love, she felt sure he cared for her. Surely love would follow, as her mother had suggested.

It wasn't difficult for Pelham to maneuver his willing fiancée onto the terrace and tempt her into a stroll in the Malcolms' garden. Some part of Pelham wanted to know the answer to the question Elspeth had raised in his mind. What would Davida's response be to a truly passionate kiss?

She giggled and came willingly into his arms when he pulled her off the lighted path and into the shadows. At first he kissed her as he always had, gently rocking his lips over hers until she melted against him. Then he deepened the kiss. At the touch of his tongue she opened her mouth almost instinctively. When he plunged inside, she was startled. For an instance she stiffened, and then on a long, shuddering breath opened fully to his exploration. When he finally pulled away, breathing heavily, she was gasping for breath, too, her nostrils flaring with passion. She clung to him, weak-kneed.

"Oh, Davida, what you do to me."

"*I* do to *you*!" She snapped, mock-indignant. "I like that. You kiss me almost senseless, then accuse me . . ."

"Not accuse you, my love. Praise you. You thrill me with your affectionate nature. I can't tell you how much I look forward to our wedding night." He pressed her against himself, letting her know how much he desired her.

Davida was glad of the covering darkness, for her cheeks were aflame. She turned a little away. "Monty, please! How am I supposed to compose myself?" *He called me his love,* she thought, her heart soaring.

Pelham looked wildly around. "Forgive me. I almost forgot where we were." He led her to a strategically placed bench. "Sit here with me a moment and then we'll go in."

Shyly she looked up at him and nodded, and he sat

sideways, facing her, holding her hands and gently swinging them. The moon lightly gilded her dusky curls and kissed her heart-shaped face. He let his eyes roam all over her possessively. "This is a little taste of hell," he murmured.

"I beg your pardon, sirrah." She flashed those brilliant eyes at him, tossing her head.

"Yes, to have just a taste of heaven when one cannot enjoy the entire dish is a kind of hell." He grinned at her. "Let's go back in before I kiss you again."

The following morning the ladies Gresham returned to their modiste, Madame Poincarré, for what Davida devoutly hoped would be the last fitting of her come-out ball gown. This gown, so long planned, had to be refitted because she had, in the frenzy of activity of the last few weeks, lost weight.

As Madame Poincarré clucked over the changes, Davida regretted once again her mother's insistence that she wear white for this occasion. She liked it as little as she had liked her court gown and all those hideous white ostrich plumes.

But if ever a girl must be completely proper and conventional, it seemed, it must be at her coming out ball. So Davida had allowed herself to be draped in white satin, overlaid with white spider gauze. To be sure, the gown was trimmed with blue satin at the bodice, high waist, sleeves, and the hem, where the gauze was caught up in scallops with large blue rosettes. Her father had presented her with an exquisite necklace featuring sapphires to help reconcile her to the gown, which she had complained made her feel like a wedding cake.

But Davida felt considerably less grumpy now as the dress was refitted. The thought of weddings was no longer distasteful or even unsettling to her, and she daydreamed a little about her coming nuptials.

The alterations were minor, and Lady Elizabeth

arranged to have a footman pick up the gown late in the afternoon.

As they entered the carriage, Davida's mother studied her daughter's face. "I believe we will stay home tonight. We could do with a quiet evening," she suggested. Monty had already informed them that he had long since accepted an invitation to dine with his mother at the home of one of her oldest and dearest friends. Since the lady was reclusive, he had not felt comfortable requesting the inclusion of his fiancée.

Davida agreed gratefully to her mother's suggestion. With preparations for a ball and a wedding underway, in addition to a full social calendar, she was nearly exhausted. And last night, after they had returned home from the Malcolms' ball, she had been unable to sleep for reliving, over and over, that astonishing kiss that Monty had given her.

She wished she could discuss the sensations it had caused in her body with her mother, but she had a notion that it had been a very improper kiss, and was afraid to broach the subject.

On the way home from the modiste, they called on Sarah, to see what progress was being made with the ball. The duke's very capable secretary had come to town two weeks earlier to open the Harwood mansion and see to any redecorating that was needed.

When the Greshams were announced in Lady D'Alatri's drawing room, they found a very downcast Lady Sarah awaiting them. "What is the matter," Davida asked, rushing to her friend's side.

"My father writes that he is not coming to London for the ball, after all." All of Sarah's usual bounce was gone; she was the picture of dejection.

Lady Elizabeth let out an exclamation of dismay. Sarah's aunt nodded her head vigorously. "It is just too bad of Justin. It is understandable that he hates the mansion where his wife died. It has such unhappy associations for him. But he has a daughter. He owes her something!"

With heavy hearts the women completed plans for decorating the ballroom in flowers that would echo the ducal colors of blue and cream. Streamers of silk in the same colors would drape from the ceiling, and be hung with shimmering silver stars. It was not the most original decorating scheme in the world, but Sarah had had little interest in anything elaborate, and the Greshams had been forced to follow her lead.

After completing their conference, the ladies sadly departed, Lady Elizabeth exclaiming over the duke's defection all the way home. "It is just wrong, for Sarah's sake. And then—gracious! The Prince Regent is coming. How will it look to him?"

When they reached the Gresham home, Davida's mother headed straight for her father's study and poured out the tale to him. Davida stood in the doorway, listening. Her mother told the story almost as if her father could do something about it.

To her amazement, Sir Charles behaved as if he could, too. "That won't do, won't do at all. He shall have to come. One doesn't invite one's sovereign to a ball and then not show. Send Robert to me."

Chapter Eighteen

As the groomsman was summoned, Davida watched her father scrawl a hasty letter, sand it, and seal it with a flourish. Her mother silently crossed the room and sat in an ancient but comfortable overstuffed chair, watching her husband as he penned a second, shorter note.

Davida sank into a chair beside her mother and listened as he instructed Robert to go to the duke's secretary. "This note will instruct him to let you have a fast horse. You are to ride as quickly as possible to Harwood Court. Here, take this purse—hire fresh horses as needed. I'm hoping you can be there by tomorrow morning. No later than midday. Can you do that?"

Robert's eyes were shining. The opportunity to ride prime bits of blood neck or nothing about the countryside obviously appealed to him. "Yes, sir. Indeed I can, sir. And am I to await a response?"

"No. The duke himself shall bring the response."

A silence descended on the three as they watched Robert jauntily walk from the room.

"George, I hope you have not done anything outrageous. The duke . . ."

"I've known Justin since he was an unlicked cub. If I can not tell him a few home truths, I don't know who can."

"He's always respected you, dear, and rightly so. Still, he can be quite stiff-necked at times."

"That's as may be. Let's have tea, I'm famished."

Davida watched in some awe as her father dismissed with a wave of his hand the Duke of Harwood. He might indeed have known him since he was an "unlicked cub," but today the duke was an urbane, sophisticated, and somewhat enigmatic person, and Davida could not imagine telling him what to do. Still, she wished her father success, for Sarah's sake if for no other reason. Fancy your own father not attending your come-out ball!

As the date of Davida and Sarah's ball approached, they were engulfed in a whirlwind of activity, of constant to-ing and fro-ing from the Greshams' home to Lady D'Alatri's, to the ducal mansion. In addition to his secretary, the duke had sent his own capable French chef, who was coordinating the contributions of the Gresham and D'Alatri kitchens, plus those of caterers. Decorators must be supervised, link-boys hired, and Gresham and D'Alatri servants fitted out in Harwood livery in order to assist at the ball.

Once it became known that the Prince Regent was attending, acceptances that had been withheld came pouring in. Also, at her father's suggestion Monty had given Davida a list of relations and special friends of his to invite. Thus the already large guest list expanded. If all came who accepted, it was going to be a squeeze, even in the duke's palatial ballroom. Davida was a little overwhelmed by the prospect, but Pelham was gleeful. "What a triumph, love. You'll be a *succes fou,* and deservedly so!"

"A mad success. Yes, if I don't go mad with these frantic preparations," she tossed back.

Just then an urgent message came to them from Sarah. They were in the Greshams' morning room, completing the place cards for the dinner to be served to intimate friends before the ball began. Pelham had willingly offered his assistance in writing them and in planning the seating. He was much more knowledgeable about who took precedence over whom, and who should be seated far apart to prevent hostilities from breaking out.

Their task was made that much more complicated because they had to make up two seating plans, one if the duke attended, and one if he didn't. "Thank goodness Prinny didn't accept for dinner, too," Pelham said with a chuckle as they discussed the complex problem.

"What can Sarah want, I wonder? And why did she not just come here?" Davida shoved an errant lock off her forehead, feeling rather put-upon.

"We'll soon know. Come, we'll walk. The exercise will do us both good, and we will get there before we could have the horses put to the carriage." After informing her mother, who was diligently addressing wedding invitations, Davida walked out with Pelham, smiling with pleasure at the sun and fair skies.

At Lady D'Alatri's, they found Sarah and her aunt entertaining a distinguished-looking young man who introduced himself as an equerry in the service of the Prince Regent. He had come to instruct them on the protocol involved in entertaining His Royal Highness. The women listened with eager faces, Davida making notes as he talked. Pelham leaned back in his chair, swinging one leg over the other and looking very amused.

After the equerry left, Davida took him to task. "Just what did you find so humorous, sirrah?"

"Ah, forgive me. My republican tendencies are showing. All this folderol about precedence and protocol. How I envy the Americans!"

Sarah was uninterested in Pelham's political views at the moment. "Wasn't he the handsomest creature you've ever seen?"

Eyebrows raised, Davida and Lady D'Alatri stared at Sarah. She had paid no attention at all to any of the dozens of young men who had attempted to court her.

"Gregory had best look to his mettle," Davida said with a laugh.

"Perhaps he had! He's not even written me, and I've written him almost every day. And that Lord Meade is all the crack! Handsome and well spoken, and with influence, too. Just think of working directly with the Prince Regent!"

Pelham laughed. "A third son, Sarah, his title is merely honorary. If his family was not so plump in the pocket, he'd be training for a parson or a soldier."

Heatedly Sarah snapped, "I don't care about that! What matters is that he's so . . . polite and, well, kind."

"Too bad it is so late in the game, I would write Gregory Allensby and tell him to get up here to protect his interests!" Davida laughed. "But the ball is tomorrow night."

Cast down, Sarah nodded. "And Gregory has never bothered to reply to my invitation."

The day of the ball dawned as clear and as beautiful as the one before. Lady Elizabeth insisted that Davida have an easy day, sleeping late and spending most of her time on grooming, so as to be rested for the ball.

Davida donned her gown that evening with trepidation, hoping she had not lost any more weight. To her relief, it still fit quite perfectly. Her sapphire necklace solaced her for the white dress. Her hair was artfully arranged by the hairdresser hired for the occasion. He had fashioned a dainty circlet of blue-and-white flowers similar to those decorating the ballroom, and fit it skillfully among her dark curls. "*Parfaítement,*" he exclaimed in a very phony French accent. "*Vous est très adorable.*"

Her maid seconded the opinion. "Oh, yes, miss. It is just right for you. Simple, yet elegant."

Davida smiled. "Well, I hope I will do." She turned around in front of her mirror, and privately thought she looked very fine, indeed.

Pelham apparently agreed. When he called for her and her parents to go to the ducal mansion for dinner, he whispered in her ear, "Exquisite." She smiled up at him, her spirits high.

They received a further boost when Sarah met them at the door, crowing, "Papa has come after all. He just arrived two hours ago. He will be down shortly."

Most of the dinner guests were assembled by the time the duke joined them. He looked, as usual, like the very pattern card of a duke. If there were lines of strain around his eyes and in the set of his mouth, only those who knew him best were aware of them. As Davida drew Monty over to introduce the two, she felt a pang of sympathy. Her father's old friend had been forced at last to return to the house where his wife had died, and it was clearly costing him.

But nothing of this showed in his manner as he acknowledged Pelham politely. Turning to Davida, one eyebrow arched, he said, "Then I take it I am not to have to marry you after all?"

Davida was surprised to find that he did indeed remember his teasing remark. She grinned pertly at him. "No, Your Grace. Are you not vastly relieved?"

"Vastly," Harwood intoned dryly. "But you are a fortunate young man, Pelham, as I hope you know."

"Indeed I do, Your Grace, I thank you."

At that moment dinner was announced. Pelham's table arrangement seemed to work, as all went smoothly, and the elaborate meal was much praised. By the time it was over, it was time to take up their places in the receiving line for the ball, so the men did not linger over their port.

Davida had smiled so much her cheeks ached by the time she had greeted, it seemed, the entire *ton* except the Prince and his party. They were not expected to arrive until after supper.

At last the duke suggested that they go in. The ball would be opened by himself and Sir Charles, dancing with their daughters in a minuet. Davida had been practicing the stately older dance so as not to disgrace herself, and from that moment until the supper dance never knew a moment's rest, as partner after partner claimed her.

The supper dance was a waltz, and she went happily into Pelham's arms. "What did I tell you, love? *Un succes fou!*" he whispered triumphantly as he whirled her around.

"Oh, I do hope so. At least it is a squeeze. If Prinny does not appear, we shall be in the suds."

"He rarely fails to show when he has committed himself, I'm told. I'm pleased to see you've changed your mind. You were upset when he first accepted, I seem to recall."

"Well, it is a little daunting, entertaining the one who is, to all purposes, one's sovereign. I was afraid I'd make a mull of it."

"Never did I doubt your ability to cope." Pelham smiled down at her. "You will make a fine political wife, though Prinny may be less than pleased to find you on the Whig side. I shall rely on you to turn him up sweet. Perhaps we can return him to the Whig fold."

Davida shook her head. "If I can just get through without disgracing myself, I shall be relieved."

Pelham smiled tenderly. "You underestimate yourself. But I was funning, actually. I don't want you having anything more to do with that old libertine than absolutely necessary."

The train of thought this engendered made Davida's pink cheeks rosier than ever, and she looked away in embarrassment—to see Lady Elspeth standing at the edge of the dance floor, staring at them. "Oh!" She missed a step.

"What is it?"

"When did she arrive? I hadn't supposed she would attend."

Pelham followed her gaze and then snorted. "Elspeth

stay away form the ball of the season, with Prinny coming? How little you know her! Do you dislike it?"

Davida looked up at him. "Of course not. I know we must meet often. It would be unwise of me to let my sensibilities be affected."

"Wise as well as beautiful." He gave her a swift whirl just as the music was ending, then led her from the floor with a flourish.

Sarah's face glowed with pleasure as she and her father welcomed Davida to their table. Her pleasure was partly for the success of the ball, but mostly because beside her was Gregory Allensby, who had come up with the duke for the ball. A shy, quiet young man, he had not joined them until the party was in full swing.

Before the second half of the ball began, Davida and Sarah decided to go to the withdrawing room set aside for the ladies. They found the room a very busy place as young and not-so-young women put hair to rights or touched up cheeks with pinches or rouge. Just as they were leaving, Lady Elspeth entered. She rushed up to Davida. "Miss Gresham, I must have a word with you."

Alarmed, Davida replied, "We cannot, not here."

"Come with me, then. There is a small study just this way." Davida reluctantly followed, ignoring Sarah's hissed advice to refuse. When she entered the room behind Elspeth, the latter turned on her. "You promised me you would break off with him. You promised!"

"I said I would if it was what he wanted, Lady Elspeth. But he doesn't. He insisted we continue our engagement. We are to be married in . . ."

"I know when, but you mustn't. He loves *me,* I tell you! I went to see him the day after the Duke of Ormond's ball, to tell him you were willing to cry off. He refused to allow it. He told me it would be dishonorable and might damage your chances of making a match. He didn't want to hurt you. His very words were, 'I could never do anything so shabby to Davida.' "

A wave of agony washed over Davida. Was Elspeth telling the truth? Before she could think of a reply, the door burst open behind them. Pelham entered swiftly, followed by Lady Howard and Sarah. Elspeth retreated a step. "Come, dear," her mother said in a tone that indicated she would take no refusal. "Your partner is looking for you for this dance."

Pelham glared at her retreating form as Elspeth left the room, eyes downcast. "What did she say to you?"

"She wants me to cry off."

"The devil! You'll do no such thing. I take it you told her?"

Just then the music suddenly stopped, and a fanfare was heard. "Oh, no, the Prince!" With Pelham right behind her, Davida fairly flew to the front of the house, finding her place in the receiving line just in time. She watched His Royal Highness greet the Duke of Harwood, exclaim with pleasure over his daughter, whom he pronounced lovely, and then greet her father. "Sir Charles, it is a pleasure. I remember reading your name in the dispatches when I was a youngster trying to learn my future duties. A brave soldier!"

Obviously pleased, Sir Charles gave him another deep bow, then presented his wife and daughter to the rotund Prince. "Enchanting," the Regent exclaimed as her mother sank into her deepest court curtsy. "I am sorry I have not met your family before, Sir Charles." He raised her mother, looking her over with pleasure as he did so.

Davida, still somewhat breathless, also curtsied deeply and then smiled as the Prince, all affability, raised her. "I must have a dance with each of these three ladies," he informed them. "Lady Sarah, will you do me the honor?"

Davida watched in awe as the Prince led her friend onto the dance floor. The Prince signified that the duke should join them, so he gave his arm to Lady Elizabeth and the four began a minuet. After several moments other dancers joined, and Davida turned to Pelham, limp with relief. "Thank you for rescuing me, Monty. What a disgrace if I had missed his entrance."

"I would like to wring Elspeth's neck, but I shall do something much better, which is ignore her entirely." Pelham's brow knit as if worried. "I hope that aging roué doesn't ask you to waltz with him."

"Monty, you can't be jealous of the Prince! And I don't think you should speak of him so. He is all that is kind."

"Oh, I don't deny that he can be charming. Too charming, in spite of his girth!"

They quarreled amiably until the dance was over. The Prince then led her mother into a set for a quadrille. Davida's partner was Threlbourne. "A smashing ball, Davida. And you look absolutely radiant." Gil's freckled countenance was lit with pleasure at her success.

"Thank you, Gil. It is so much different from what I expected. To think a few short weeks ago I knew hardly anyone in London."

"And now the cream of the *ton* is here in your honor. You'll be quite unbearable."

She dimpled up at him. " 'Tis every young lady's dream—to be such a success she can be unbearable!"

"And yet you won't be. You are too fine a person." Gil looked at Pelham, further along in the set with another partner. "Hope he appreciates you."

Remembering Elspeth's words, Davida suppressed a little shudder.

"What's wrong?"

"Somebody walked on my grave, I think."

"Now, none of that. Let me tell you about the new team I've just purchased."

"Another one?"

Before she knew it, Davida was standing up with the Prince, and it was a waltz. Casting a quick glance at Pelham, who was frowning on the sideline, Davida smiled

up at her sovereign as she turned with him. He was surprisingly agile and light on his feet, considering his size,
and charming as well.

He began by praising her mother's beauty in fulsome
terms that left Davida somewhat uneasy. The Regent's
penchant for mature ladies was quite openly discussed in
ton drawing rooms. How terrible it would be if the
Prince developed a *tendre* for her mother.

Her mind continued in this alarming whirl when the
Prince went on to boast of her father's war record. "We
need loyal Tories like him. Backbone of the realm. I'm
going to try to persuade him to stand for Parliament."

Davida tried to imagine her home-loving country
farmer of a father as a member of the House of Com-
mons, but she couldn't. Baffled, she gave her head a little shake. "I would be truly amazed if he should do so,
but he certainly casts his vote for our Tory member, as
you may well know."

After the dance, the Prince led her to her parents and
Pelham, and chatted with them for a while. He invited
them all to join him in Brighton for the summer. The invitation was general, but his eyes were on Lady Elizabeth. Davida's mother calmly deferred to her husband,
who excused them on the grounds that he was involved
in an extensive project to drain a marsh.

With an inward sigh of relief Davida realized that her
father was more than able to fend off the Prince Regent's
interest in his wife.

As for Pelham, he thanked the Prince graciously for
his invitation, but indicated that he had already planned
an extensive honeymoon to be spent showing Davida
around his various estates.

The Prince took the refusals affably, and after a few
more minutes of trivial conversation, left the dance. The
rest of the ball went by in a happy blur, and it was an exhausted Miss Davida Gresham who returned to her home

and fell into her bed almost the minute the maid took off
her gown.

She fell asleep immediately, but awoke with a start
early in the morning from a terrible dream in which Pelham and Elspeth were dancing together as Davida
watched. In her dream everyone was staring at her ac-
cusingly and saying, "A shabby thing, a shabby thing,"
over and over.

As she lay there trying to shake the unpleasant dream
and get back to sleep, Elspeth's words came back to
taunt her. She seemed so utterly convinced that the only
thing keeping Pelham in their engagement was a sense
of honor. She had quoted him as saying it would be
shabby to cry off. Did that mean he wished to do so?
Was Pelham only pretending to be happy about their engagement?

She sighed and sank back into the covers. Surely no
one could pretend so well, and so long. She could swear
he felt some affection for her. But what did he feel for
Elspeth? Perhaps nothing, as he claimed. But the very
passion with which he expressed his anger toward her
suggested otherwise. People rarely wanted to wring the
necks of those for whom they felt nothing.

Eventually, sleep reclaimed her, but not before she
had firmly made up her mind to dwell only on the pleasant memories of the success of her come-out ball. Any
presentiments of trouble were firmly suppressed.

Chapter Nineteen

Davida and Monty were to be wed on the first Wednesday after the third and final crying of the banns. Their last ball as an engaged couple was to be the Raleigh ball, held on Friday at the Raleighs' palatial country estate just an hour's drive from London. It was to be a huge event, with everyone who was anyone being invited.

The Raleighs liked to entertain on a grand scale, so not only the ball room, but several drawing rooms and card rooms were filled to capacity indoors. The extensive gardens had been decorated with fairy lanterns, and refreshment tents had been set up to hold the overflow, as not all could possibly fit in the dining rooms.

As Pelham escorted Davida through the crowds, he contemplated the gardens beyond the windows with pleasure. "We must go outside after we have danced awhile. Mayhap we can find a dark path in the garden, and . . ." He raised his eyebrows suggestively, and Davida felt that surge of warmth that so often overcame her around her fiancé. "Sounds delightful," she murmured, giving him a dreamy smile.

Her response kindled a warm glow in his cobalt eyes. "Indeed, I think we should plan to meet out there, for we are likely to be separated in this crush. As I recall, there is a large fountain at the center of the garden, with dozens of nymphs sporting in the water. If I don't make it to your side when they begin the supper dance, have your partner bring you there. We'll take supper in one of the tents."

As he predicted, they were separated in the crush after the first dance. Davida's mother found a comfortable chair among the other chaperons, and her father retreated to the card room. A steady stream of dance partners kept Davida happily entertained, though she would have preferred to be with Monty.

A brief meeting with Lady Elspeth caused her a few moments of uneasiness. Monty's erstwhile fiancée stared her up and down and demanded, "Where is Lord Pelham? I am surprised you let him out of your sight, Miss Gresham. The two of you have become inseparable. Do you not fear never to find him again in this crush?"

Davida wasn't sure how to respond. There were several people listening, doubtless eager to turn into scandal any hint of animosity. So she just laughed and said, "We're meeting at the central fountain in the garden for supper. I'm sure he will manage without me for that long."

Pelham tired of dancing and the crowds and found his way to the fountain in time to blow a cloud before supper. As he stood contemplating the drifting couples all around him, some of them exploring the quieter walkways as he meant to do soon with Davida, he heard his name called.

He turned, irritated, for he recognized the voice. "Lady Elspeth." He bowed formally but his stance was wary. "Surprised to see you here without an escort."

"I wanted to speak to you privately for a moment."

"I really have nothing to say to you, Elspeth, at least nothing you would take any pleasure in hearing." He gave her a stern, hard look. "I said it all that day in my library."

"I want us to cry friends, Monty." Elspeth walked out

of the darkened path behind him. "Can we not at least be friends?"

"Of course." His expression softened. "I would like that, Elspeth."

"Are you enjoying the ball?"

"These sad crushes are beginning to be just a bit tiresome, I must admit." Pelham started to turn around to search the walkway leading from the mansion for Davida, but Elspeth stopped him with an urgent, "Wait!"

"What is it, Elspeth?" He turned back to her reluctantly. "I must watch for Davida. She is to meet me here."

"I'd best leave before she arrives. Let us shake hands, Monty." She held her hand out to him.

Davida had danced every dance, and by the time the supper dance was announced, she was exhausted. She was promised to Gilbert, and when the redheaded viscount found her, she turned to him eagerly.

"Gil, my feet feel like stumps! Do let us pass this one up. I am to join Monty in the garden at the end of it anyway."

"Naughty, naughty!" Gilbert's grin was teasing rather than condemning, which didn't for one second relieve the blushes that sprang so readily to Davida's cheeks.

"Beast! We're going to get our supper in one of the tents. It's far too stuffy in here, and too crowded as well."

"I'll certainly agree to that." He helped her maneuver through the crowds and out the massive French doors which opened onto the elaborate garden.

"That was the simple part. Which fountain?"

As they stood looking out over the terraced scene, they could see the tops of dozens of fountains above the lush shrubbery. "Oh, my!" Davida wracked her brain. "I think he said it was near the center, and there were nymphs . . ."

They moved down the garden paths, peering to right and left. "Lost?" A deep voice that she recognized too well caused Davida to jump. "Or getting in practice for a true *ton* marriage?"

Gilbert chose to ignore the suggestive comment. "I say, Harry. You wouldn't know the way to the central fountain, would you? The one with all of the nymphs?"

"Yes, but I'm not sure you should take *Miss* Gresham there." Though he gave his usual emphasis to the "Miss," there was nothing sportive about Curzon's tone.

"Do give over, Harry. You know good and well . . . just escorting Davida to Monty."

"My point exactly." Curzon looked enigmatically at the two irritated, puzzled people before him. "Ah, well, tried to warn you. Continue along this path, then turn to the left when it crosses the next by the Apollo fountain."

Davida looked behind her after they passed Curzon. He was standing still, watching them, a brooding look on his face. A sense of foreboding filled her.

It was a sense that was fully justified as they continued down the indicated path. Ahead of them was the nymph fountain, and as they rounded it they came upon Monty, his back to them, deep in conversation with Elspeth and oblivious to their approach.

Gilbert swore softly; Davida couldn't make out his words but fully entered into his feelings, for just then Monty took Elspeth's hand, then jerked her into his arms and kissed her. Moments later he pushed her from him almost violently.

Davida stopped in her tracks, an unwilling audience to this meeting between Elspeth and Monty. What she saw and heard was not calculated to give comfort to his current fiancée.

When Pelham took Elspeth's hand to shake it, she grasped his firmly, then suddenly tugged sharply on it, at the same time bringing her other arm up to curve around his neck. Caught off balance, Pelham had to grab her firmly to keep from falling.

Straining upward, she brought her lips to his. He registered her womanly curves and her warmth, and for an instant he held her, his mouth softening on hers. Then he pulled away, setting her firmly at arm's length.

"Kiss me one more time, Monty," she whispered. And then, louder, a harsh sound to her voice, "Kiss me the way you did that day in your library."

Startled by her actions, Pelham stood motionless for a few moments. In a low voice he demanded, "What May Game is this? I told you . . ."

"Yes, I know." Her voice grew louder. "You told me that you cannot let Davida cry off. As you said, it would be a shabby thing to do, no matter how much you wish it. Our love must go unrequited. But won't you give me one last kiss?"

"We had our last kiss the day after you jilted Whitham. I told you then, and I tell you now—you must accept it. I am going to marry Davida, no matter . . ."

Pelham didn't get a chance to continue, because suddenly Elspeth, who was positioned so that she could see the walkway, gasped, "Davida. How long have you been . . . Oh, dear. We were just . . . that is, wc were just saying good-bye. Please don't be upset at Monty."

Pelham spun around to see Davida's white, unhappy face as she stared at the pair. Just behind her stood Viscount Threlbourne, looking very indignant.

"I knew it. . . . I knew it. . . ." Davida began backing away.

"Wait, Davie, I can explain."

"No, Monty, let her go. This has gone on long enough." Gil took Davida by the shoulders and turned her, nudging her back down the garden walkway. "You and Elspeth have kissed and made up. Be done with it. Davida is better off with a broken engagement than an unhappy marriage."

He blocked Pelham's path while Davida fled up the walkway as if all the fiends of hell were on her heels. When Pelham tried to shake free of his friend, Elspeth grasped his arm, her small hands surprisingly strong as she clung to his coat. "Let her go, let her go. As Gil says, it's for the best. Now she'll cry off and we can be wed."

People were staring at Monty and Elspeth, and at Davida's hastily retreating figure. Pelham turned back and firmly detached Elspeth's hands. "You are making a fool of yourself before all the *ton*, Lady Elspeth. Kindly don't include me in your folly."

"But it's me you love. I know it is!"

He looked down at her and realized that he could quite honestly deny any love for her. All he felt was disgust with his former fiancée and concern about Davida. "No, Lady Elspeth. Any slight remnants of feelings I had for you have been quite completely destroyed by this charade. You knew Davida was listening, didn't you? You deliberately gave her a false impression. Dishonest, cruel creature! I have done with you, once and for all!" He turned his back on her tears without a qualm.

Hearing this speech, Gilbert braced him by the arms while looking at him questioningly. "Get out of my way, Threlbourne."

"Did you mean what you said to Elspeth just now?"

"With all my heart. Now move!"

Gilbert allowed himself to be thrust aside, and turned to soothe Elspeth's tears.

As quickly as he could without attracting more attention, Pelham hurried up the walkway, frantically searching for Davida. But she had disappeared into the throngs, and his search was in vain.

When Davida had last seen her parents, they were in the card room nearest the ballroom. With unseemly haste she pushed her way through the crowd and hurried to them. "Take me home," she gasped.

"Why, Davida, darling, what is it?" Her mother, alarmed, rose from the table.

"Take me home now. Please, Papa, before I disgrace us all!"

The look on her face convinced her father. He stood, excusing himself, and began escorting the two women toward the front of the mansion. "But what of Lord Pelham?" he asked.

"He will find his own way home. Doubtless Lady Elspeth will take him up." Her pain and grief were in her face. The bitterness in her tone caused the Greshams to exchange alarmed glances.

Once they were settled in their carriage and under way, Davida stammered out a tearful account of what she had seen and heard in the garden. "He jerked her into his arms and kissed her. I heard her saying he wouldn't let me cry off because it was a shabby thing to do. He didn't deny it. He just told her she must accept it."

Her mother's response was ready sympathy. She put her arms around her sobbing daughter and rocked her like a baby.

Her father sat back in the carriage, his face stony and unreadable in the dim light. When Davida had cried out her first rush of grief, she lifted her head.

"I can't marry him now, Papa, you do see that. It is as I feared all along. He still loves her. He regrets proposing to me. Shabby. Shabby! He won't let me cry off because it wouldn't be proper. But he would always regret it. Oh, Papa, don't you see. He'll be miserable, and so will I."

At last her father spoke. "She is a schemer. I believe she arranged for you to see them together."

"Yes," Davida admitted. "I expect she did plan it. She knew I was meeting him there. But it was clear that she was repeating what he had said to her. And I saw him take her into his arms. I saw him kiss her. Perhaps they planned it together."

"I can't believe that of Lord Pelham," her father growled.

Lady Elizabeth sighed. "Nor can I. He seems too honorable a man for that."

"You're right, of course. He is. He is also too honorable to break off with me now, no matter how much he may want to. But I can and I will. I won't be married to a man who loves another woman."

"Careful, daughter. We haven't heard from him yet. I would like to hear his explanation first."

Near hysterics, Davida shrieked, "I heard all I needed to hear tonight. I won't marry him."

"Calm yourself, Davida. Your father won't force you . . ."

"Madam, please do not speak for me. I will do what is best in the long run for my daughter, not give in to feminine hysterics. An engagement broken four days before the wedding will be an embarrassment to Lord Pelham, but he will overcome it. But Davida, we are not high enough in the *ton* to flaunt its standards. You'll never recover from it. Your hopes of a good marriage—perhaps any marriage at all—will be dashed."

"I'd rather not marry, then."

"And I am convinced Pelham will make you a good husband in spite of . . ."

"No!"

"And you care deeply for him. Deny it if you can."

"I do love him. Which is why I *won't* marry him."

Angrily father and daughter faced each other across the carriage.

"You'll do as I say, daughter."

"Papa!"

"Charles, please . . ."

"Quiet! Let's not share this with the servants." The

carriage had stopped and the footman was opening the door.

Silently the three trooped into the entryway. "Go to bed, Davida. We will talk more of this tomorrow." Her father's face was so set and stern that Davida felt her spirits sink completely.

"Yes, Papa," she whispered, stumbling up the steps until her mother joined her and put a steadying arm around her. She barely heard her mother's soothing words. There had been something implacable in her father's face.

She allowed herself to be undressed and put to bed like a doll. But after the candle had been extinguished, Davida lay sleepless, her mind as busy as her body was still. Endlessly she went over her relationship with Montgomery Villars, seeking any hint that he might truly care for her, but finding nothing that could convince her. She found, to her intense dismay, plenty of evidence of lust, but that was not love.

Painfully she faced the fact that time and time again she had looked the other way, refusing to see the evidence of her eyes and ears, refusing to face the truth of her own instincts, because she wanted to stay engaged to Pelham.

Again and again her mind returned to the scene in the Malcolm's garden. It had haunted her since it happened. To remember that deep, intimate kiss always filled her with contradictory emotions, a fiery tingling, and yet a shuddering, shivery sensation, too. She didn't know how to interpret what it made her feel, except that she wanted to feel that way again.

But tonight as she thought of it, she cringed with shame and self-disgust. She had let him kiss her that way and hadn't even protested. She had let him press himself against her and had wanted more. And all the time he was doubtless wishing it was Elspeth he held, Elspeth he kissed.

As she recalled what had been said in the Raleighs'
garden tonight, she realized that he had admitted to kissing Elspeth on the very day he had assured her that his
love for Elspeth was gone. It had been that very evening
that he had kissed Davida so intimately in the Malcolms'
garden.

It had seemed right to her because she loved him. But
to him it must have been merely an expression of lust
and, yes, of mastery. He knew his power over her. Any-
time she expressed her misgivings, he seemed to kiss
them away.

Davida thought of all the gossip she had heard about
affairs among members of the *ton*. Perhaps Pelham
thought he could have both of them. Perhaps he planned
to make Elspeth his lover as soon as they all were safely
wed. That kind of marriage seemed to be what Curzon
had been hinting at in the garden. The very thought of it
filled her with revulsion. Somehow she had to escape
this doomed marriage that would make them both miserable.

For a long while her thoughts went in circles, but suddenly, somewhere in that ambiguous hour just before
dawn, the solution came to her.

She knew her father's fears that she'd never make another match half so good were justified. Nor did she
truly want any husband but Pelham. But the only way
her father would permit her to cry off was if she had a
better match.

Unknown to him, she'd already been offered a better
match, in the worldly sense, at least. Her mind went
back to the day she and Sarah had modeled two of their
new gowns for Sarah's father, on the eve of their departure for London.

As she had twirled about for the duke, her jonquil yellow sprigged muslin flaring out from its high waist, he
had stared, seemingly stunned. When she stopped to
look up into his face quizzically, he had seemed almost

to shake himself before drawling in his ironical way, "You've become a lovely woman, Davida. I've a mind to marry you myself. If you don't find a suitable husband in London, remember that you have a devoted suitor, right here in your home county."

Davida had laughed and blushed and had thought little of it. But Sarah, reminding her of it after the breakup with Curzon, had said she thought her father was serious. He would be lonely when Sarah married, and he'd want a woman to run his household, too, wouldn't he?

What was it he had said at her come-out ball? Oh, yes. He had agreed that he was relieved not to have to marry her. But had there had been something in his manner, in his eyes . . . ? And hadn't he told Pelham how fortunate he was?

Almost forty, the duke would surely not be looking for anything from a wife but companionship. That Davida could offer him. And her father certainly couldn't complain if she were to become a duchess!

But the Duke of Harwood had returned to his country estate the day following the ball. He couldn't stand to remain in the town mansion where his wife had died one second longer than necessary. Somehow, she would have to get Harwood Court if she was to ask him to marry her.

As dawn crept slowly into the sky, Davida rose from her bed, dressed in a sensible carriage dress, packed a portmanteau, and retrieved what remained of her quarter's allowance from the top drawer of her dressing table.

From her jewelry box she took a few small items that might supplement her money in case of an emergency, trying not to look at the box containing the Pelham emeralds which she had donned so proudly last night. They could be returned later, she thought as she locked the jewelry box again. Doubtless they would be perfect to set off Elspeth's green eyes!

She silently slipped down the stairs. Muted sounds

told her the servants had begun their day's work in the kitchen, but none were in view as she padded as quietly as possible to the front door, threw the bolt, and let herself out.

Chapter Twenty

"Gone? Where?" Lord Pelham stood aghast in the Greshams' morning room, facing her anxious parents. He looked as if he hadn't slept all night. He had tried unsuccessfully to catch up to Davida when she fled from him, and by the time he had been able to arrange transportation from the ball, the Greshams' home was dark. He had decided to wait until morning to go to Davida and explain.

Racing up the steps to the Gresham town house long before the fashionable hour, he had been astonished to find the door open and the servants standing about like lost souls. Perry had finally noticed him and stepped forward. "Miss Davida . . . isn't below, my lord. Shall I direct you to her parents?"

Now he stood shocked in the Greshams' morning room, where a red-eyed Lady Elizabeth dabbed at her nose while Sir Charles held a sheet of paper out to him.

"She didn't leave us a note, but she left one for you. I took the liberty of opening it. I felt my daughter's safety demanded it."

"Yes, of course." Pelham hastily opened the folded sheet and read its contents.

Dear Lord Pelham:
   It is as I feared. You are obviously still very much in love with Lady Elspeth. Our engagement has become an obstacle to your happiness.

As my father does not seem likely to permit me to withdraw quietly from the match, I have decided to terminate it in a way he won't refuse—by contracting a more favorable match as soon as may be.

I wish you and your lady all happiness and hope we may remain friends.

                              Your Obedient and Humble etc.
                              Davida Gresham

Pelham cleared his emotion-choked throat. "What does she mean, a more favorable match? Was there another offer she was considering?"

Sir Charles shook his head. "The only suitor I know of that she was seriously considering was Mr. Curzon. But she took him in dislike at the end. Other offers there were, but none that were both suitable and acceptable to Davida."

"Perhaps she went to Curzon, then." Pelham frowned at the thought.

"I think mayhap she has. I've ordered my carriage around."

"May I accompany you, sir?"

"Indeed, I hope you will. Or . . . I say, *do* you wish the match to be broken off?"

"Certainly not."

"You're not so hen-hearted as to marry out of a sense of honor, if you truly love another woman? I hope you will be honest with us, for Davida's sake as well as your own."

"I do believe at this late date it would be dishonorable to cry off." Pelham ran a hand distractedly through his auburn hair. "Still, I wouldn't marry Davida if it were really Elspeth I wanted. I swear to you it's not. As for last night, far from realizing that I still love her, I have seen her revealed as a person of very low character, in addition to having a temperament I never could endure."

"Ah! I suspected as much. But Davida must have it

that you were consumed with love for her, and simply couldn't honorably break the engagement."

"Consumed with fury, more like! The bit—excuse me, Lady Elizabeth, the jade! What Davida saw and overheard last night was a deliberate plot on Elspeth's part to drive my fiancée to cry off."

"We'd guessed as much," Lady Elizabeth said. "But Davida simply couldn't bear the thought of making you unhappy."

Just then Perry's round face appeared in the doorway. "The carriage is at the ready, sir."

"Good. Wait here, m'dear, we should know something soon." Sir Charles patted his wife on the shoulder before leaving with Pelham.

Harrison Curzon stood before his early morning visitors in his dressing gown, as astonished as he was disheveled.

"Davida, here? What's happened?" Curzon's sleepy countenance became enlivened with a certain ironic amusement. "Never say she's jilted you. Becoming quite the thing this season, jilting Baron Pelham."

Too concerned to pay attention to the jibe, Pelham kept on as if he hadn't heard. "I hope we can rely upon your discretion, Harry." Sir Charles paced nervously as he listened. "Elspeth played a bit of a trick on us last night, and now Davida's gone missing. Her note said something about making an acceptable match elsewhere, and we thought perhaps . . ."

"Good God, no! Even if she had come here, I wouldn't want second place in her life any more than she wants it in yours. Can't say I blame her. Damn all, Pelham. You should never have offered for her. Now you've hurt her. I should call you out for this!"

Angrily Pelham retorted, "I am at your service! Speaking of hurting her, perhaps you would like to explain why she trembles with fear whenever she comes near you?"

In a steely voice that reminded both young men that he had once been a commanding officer, Sir Charles brought them to attention. "That will do for now. You young cocks may posture and fight later, if you like, but right now the essential thing is to find Davida."

Curzon turned to Sir Charles. "Surely she has some sort of sensible plan? She's a bright gel, sir. I'm sure she hasn't come to any harm. Perhaps she's with her friend, what is her name . . . the duke's daughter?"

"Right now she's a very young, innocent girl on her own in a large, wicked city." Davida's father's voice was heavy with pain. "If you do hear anything, you'll let us know?"

"Of course. And don't worry. Won't say anything to a soul. You've my word on it." He directed his remarks to Sir Charles. "If there's any way I can aid you, let me know." They shook hands, and then the dejected father and fiancé climbed back into Sir Charles's carriage.

"Any other ideas, sir?"

"None. Of course we must see if she's at Sarah's, but her note seemed to indicate . . . 'a more favorable match.' 'A more favorable match.' " Sir Charles mused on Davida's words and then a look of horror crossed his face. "She surely wouldn't have gone to old Lord Tarkington!"

Pelham swore violently. "Never say you considered him?"

"Not for a minute, nor did Davida. But he did offer and we joked about it. About marrying her to his title." Sir Charles dropped his head in his hands in dejection. "Never really cared about the title, you know. Not really. Wanted her to be happy. Thought she would be, with you."

They drove to Sarah's aunt's home, where the servants assured them Miss Davida had not been there. In fact,

Lady Sarah and Lady D'Alatri were on their way to the Greshams'.

The two men drove silently back to the Gresham house, to find Sarah and her aunt with Lady Elizabeth in the drawing room.

"Oh, George. Sarah thinks Davida may have gone to her father!"

"Harwood? Why?"

"My father teased Davida about marrying him. Just before we left for London, he told her if she didn't find what she was looking for during the season, he'd offer for her."

"But he was joking, surely."

"Davida took it so at the time, sir, but I know my father. There was something about his manner. I felt if she'd taken him seriously, he would have been pleased. I said as much to her after she turned down Mr. Curzon."

Lady D'Alatri nodded her head. "I know my brother admires Davida very much. In the letter in which he informed me that he wasn't coming to Sarah's ball, he alluded to her engagement as an 'expected disappointment.' "

"My, my." The look in Sir Charles eyes made Pelham suddenly doubt the old knight's disdain for a title. With a chilling sense of foreboding he realized that a baron was a poor prospect if a duke was in the running.

Lady Elizabeth was anxiously looking at her husband for confirmation. "Could she have gone home, George? But how?" Suddenly she began to cry. "My baby, traveling to Queenswicke all alone."

"Now, now, mother. We'll leave immediately. That is to say . . ." Sir Charles lifted a questioning eye to Lord Pelham.

"Yes, sir, of course I'll go, but with your permission, I'll ride ahead, see if I can get some confirmation that she is traveling in that direction. I can travel much faster on horseback."

"Oh, Charles. I just know that's what she's done. I'm coming with you."

"Someone must stay here in case she returns. Sarah, Lady D'Alatri, would you keep Elizabeth company?" At Sarah's eager nod, and her aunt's murmured "of course," Sir Charles turned to Pelham. "If you can mount me, Lord Pelham, I'll ride with you instead of taking the traveling coach. Every minute may count. You can't tell what kind of villain she may run into."

Reluctantly Lady Elizabeth saw her husband off to Pelham's mews to select two of his fastest horses. Then she turned to her guests.

"You must help me keep rumor at bay. I'm sure many people noticed something odd at the ball last night. Soon all the old tabbies will be here to sniff out a scandal."

"I'm sure you are right, Cousin Elizabeth. Stories were already flying at the Raleighs' last night. That's what brought me here so early."

"We'll put it about that she has an influenza. No, perhaps just a cold. They may get her back in time for the wedding, so it must be something mild."

Lady D'Alatri agreed. "And if anyone asks about last night, you can just admit they had a lovers' tiff, but say that all is well now."

Sarah nodded enthusiastically. "And I'll say I looked in on her this morning and she could hardly speak for sneezing. We'll be very anxious for her to get well in time for the wedding."

"How shall we account for both Lord Pelham and my husband's absence?" Lady Elizabeth looked anxiously from one to the other.

Sarah tapped her toes, looking at the ceiling for inspiration. "Perhaps . . . perhaps they are with the lawyers, working to complete the settlements before the wedding?"

Davida's mother looked downcast. "Do you think there'll be a wedding? After this start, Pelham may not want her."

"Oh, Cousin Elizabeth. I think Monty cares for her very much. I shouldn't be surprised at all to find he loves her, though he may not know it yet."

"Yes, I've thought as much myself. I was quite surprised when Davida told me of his tryst with Lady Elspeth last night."

"If only . . ."

"What, Sarah dear?"

"Oh, forgive me, Cousin Elizabeth, but I was just wondering. If Sir Charles learns she could be a duchess, will he still want her to wed Lord Pelham?"

Lady Elizabeth stared at Sarah, speechless, for a long moment, then answered in a firm, determined voice. "I'm sure he'll give her a choice. He certainly won't *make* her take your father if she prefers Pelham. Not if he ever wants any peace in his own home, at least!"

Sarah smiled and hugged Lady Elizabeth. "I was hoping you'd say that. Oh, I do wonder how it will all come out."

Davida was certainly a very young, very innocent girl on her own in a wicked world. But she was also very resourceful. And even in the large, wicked world there were many decent people. She was fortunate enough to find some of them on her journey north.

When she crept into the barely gray morning, her first goal was a hackney cab stand she knew of not too far from her home. Here she found a driver dozing on his box as his horse dozed in its traces.

First he tried to talk her into returning to her home. Clearly such a well-spoken young lady had no business going about London on her own! But when she insisted, and turned to look for another cab, he relented and took her straight to the Swan With Two Necks. He didn't overcharge her on her fare and even carried her bag inside and helped her buy a ticket.

Davida knew that traveling to Queenswicke in a post

chaise would require an overnight stay, with its attendant expenses and dangers. And she was ill-equipped to do the bargaining with hostlers and postillions that would be required. If she took one of the new Fast Coaches, she could be in her little village before midnight. She decided the lack of comfort and privacy of a public coach was preferable to an overnight stay.

She soon found herself hurtling down the road at a breakneck pace, almost as fast as the famous mail coaches. Her fellow travelers were all of a lower social status than she was accustomed to dealing with. However, a plump, talkative farmer's wife soon had them all transformed from strangers into friends.

She took Davida under her wing immediately, not that she needed any protecting from the others, a young law student and a thin, sickly former soldier with only one arm.

From each of her fellow travelers the farmer's wife seemed determined to extract a story, as if planning to play Chaucer and develop her own *Canterbury Tales*. When Davida's turn came, she told an edited version of the truth, having little experience with contriving made-up stories. She found sympathy from the others, and the goodwife, Mrs. Randall, offered her something even better, the promise of a generous helping from the picnic basket she had brought.

Having had no breakfast, Davida was quite starved and very grateful. On a brief stop at a posting house, while the horses were swiftly changed, Mrs. Randall admonished her, "Don't try to buy food, you won't have time any way. We'll go to the withdrawing room to freshen up, and then purchase a jug of tea to wash down my picnic."

Davida was soon glad she had followed this excellent advice; it was astonishing how quickly the horses were changed and they were called back to the coach. She ate hard boiled eggs, thickly sliced ham, bread and fruit, all washed down with the tea as the carriage rumbled on.

"That was the best meal I've ever eaten," Davida sighed.

Mrs. Randall winked as she passed some rations to the others. "There's naught like hunger to improve the cook."

At the next, slightly longer, stop, a ribbon merchant replaced the young law clerk, who had hardly taken his rapturous gaze off Davida since she entered the coach, but had never gathered his nerve to speak to her.

The ribbon merchant, a jovial man, had Davida's story from Mrs. Randall, and insisted on buying them both a dish of tea and some scones at the next posting house. When Davida tried to demur, he wouldn't accept her refusal. "Now, miss, I'll bet you've bought many a ribbon from me indirectly, through Mr. Barstow there in Meersford. 'Tis only right that I treat ye!"

Since Davida had indeed patronized the Barstows whenever her father took them to the nearby market town, she smiled and accepted graciously.

Some miles later the ribbon merchant was replaced by a stout cleric. To Davida's relief, Mrs. Randall did not tell the runaway's story to Reverend Arksworth, who might have scolded her at the least, and even perhaps appointed himself to return her to her parents.

Instead, the worthy minister began to argue theology with the soldier, whose own religious beliefs had been shaken in the ordeal of war. Though she had firm religious beliefs, Davida was no theologian. She began to doze.

When she awoke Mrs. Randall was gently shaking her shoulder. Another stop. It was midafternoon. She made haste to freshen herself while the horses were changed. The kindly goodwife left her a bundle of bread and cheese, for this was where she would leave the coach.

By early evening the only passenger remaining from

the original group was the soldier, who was going to
visit his brother in Leiscester. He had assured Mrs. Randall he would watch out for Davida. But no one offered
her insult or danger, only a good deal of contradictory
advice while the coach thundered on.

At Queenswicke, where she had originally planned to
leave the coach to take a hackney to Harwood Court,
Davida changed her plans slightly. At the last posting
house she had caught a look at her pale face and disheveled clothing in the mirror of the refreshing room.
She looked terrible. Also, it was going to be very late by
the time she could reach the duke's. She would have to
rouse him from his slumbers. Both vanity and prudence
dictated that she look more the thing before proposing to
Lord Harwood. Also, at this late hour, it would be very
difficult to arrange transport to Harwood Court from
Queenswicke, whereas the larger town of Meersford
would readily be able to provide her with a hackney
whenever she wanted it.

Briefly, Davida considered going home, but she was
afraid that her father's servants might prove uncoopera-
tive. Old family retainers were often every bit as stuffy
and domineering as parents. The housekeeper, in particular, might cut up stiff about letting her go to visit the
Duke of Harwood on her own.

So she decided not to get off at Queenswicke, which
was too small to have a decent inn. She purchased the
additional ticket and continued to Meersford. It was not
much farther from Harwood Court than Queenswicke,
which was situated at the apex of a triangle almost
equidistant from the two towns. There, at the Boar and
Thistle, she could safely take a room for the night, for
she knew the proprietors well, having often taken tea
with her family there. She could rest a few hours, change
into a fresh dress, and catch the early rising duke before
he had time to depart on his day's activities.

It was with great relief that, near midnight, she entered the Boar and Thistle. "Miss Gresham, is it?" The surprised younger son of the innkeeper greeted her. "But whatever are you doing on a public coach? Where is your family? Never say you are traveling without a maid?"

"Hello, Paul." Davida had expected questions, but this barrage overwhelmed her. "I am exhausted. Could I have a room and a cold collation?"

"Of course, Miss Gresham. Right away."

"I'll need a gig or a hackney to take me to the Duke of Harwood's tomorrow at first light," she informed Paul as he handed her a room key.

"The duke? Not going home, hey?"

Davida had decided that the best approach with Paul and the other workers at the inn was simply not to answer their questions, so she just smiled at him. "And could I have some warm water for a bath, please?"

Davida did not expect to sleep very much, so worried as she was about her coming interview with the duke. But she had slept little the night before, and the day had been exhausting. Before she could be assailed by her doubts, or wonder what her parents were thinking, Davida had fallen soundly asleep.

Chapter Twenty-one

Lord Pelham and Sir Charles had started several hours behind Davida, but they had two distinct advantages. First, riding on prime bloods, they could make much better time than even the fastest coach.

Second, once they had learned at The Swan With Two Necks that a young girl answering Davida's description had indeed purchased a ticket for Queenswicke on the northbound Fast Coach, they could ride the coach's route with single-minded purpose, stopping only to change horses and grab a quick bite to eat. During such stops they made inquiries and were able to ascertain that Davida was still on the coach, still destined for Queenswicke.

At the last stop before Queenswicke, they verified that Davida had been seen on the coach, and decided to ride straight to Harwood Court.

"There's not a decent inn in Queenswicke," Sir Charles had reasoned, "so she'll cozen some sort of conveyance and go directly to Harwood."

They fully expected Davida to have arrived there an hour or two before them. It was 3 A.M. They had been blessed with a nearly full moon, which had made it possible for them to ride swiftly through the night.

When they at last roused the duke, they were horrified to learn that Davida had not arrived. Pelham feared that Sir Charles would collapse, so upset was he at this news.

After a reviving brandy, though, Davida's father pulled himself together.

"She must have gone home. No doubt that's what she intended all along." Sir Charles looked hopefully at Pelham for confirmation.

"Or perhaps there is someone else she might visit nearby?" Pelham's query had the same hopeful, unsure quality about it.

The Duke of Harwood was curious, but too discreet to question his obviously distraught neighbor closely. He was told only that Davida had left home having given the impression she was coming to see him.

After he had sent his tired visitors on their way to Sir Charles's nearby home, the Duke of Harwood mused over a brandy, wondering why Davida would come to him. It would be most improper. Unless? An interesting explanation caused the duke's lips to curve in a speculative smile.

At the Gresham manor house, a single question to the sleepy, astonished servant who answered the door plunged Sir Charles into despair. "Not here, Monty. Damn all! Where can the chit have gotten to?"

"Perhaps she stopped somewhere to spend the night? Probably didn't want to land on the Duke of Harwood's doorstep in the middle of the night. Probably worn to the bone, too, pounding along all day in a public coach."

Gray with exhaustion, Sir Charles could only say grimly, "I hope you are right, young man, though I have no idea who she would turn to other than Harwood. But I can't go on without a little rest. We'll start early and search for her tomorrow."

Lord Pelham wanted to go on searching, but he was unfamiliar with the country, and by this time the moon had set, making riding dangerous under the best of circumstances. He decided to rest for a few hours along with Sir Charles and then get an early start in the morning.

The first rooster was crowing as the maid obediently awakened Davida. She groaned, sure the bird must be mistaken, for she could detect no light in the sky. Still, she got up and hastily made her toilet, swallowed a dish of tea with a sweet roll, and settled into the hackney which she had requested the night before. By the time dawn was streaking the night sky, she was demanding entrance to the Duke of Harwood's home.

"The little minx!" Lord Harwood snapped when told by his sleepy and very exasperated butler that Miss Davida Gresham awaited him below. Servant and master alike had barely fallen asleep again after his first visitors had departed.

"Tell her I will be with her shortly. And send a messenger to Sir Charles immediately to let him know his lost lamb has turned up on my doorstep."

When Harwood entered his front drawing room, he paused a moment to savor the fresh beauty of his guest, who was standing like a frightened fawn before his carved marble fireplace.

"Davida, my child. This is a surprise!" Lifting her from her curtsy, he took her hands and led her to a settee. "I am sure you have a reasonable explanation for your presence here, unaccompanied, and at this barbaric hour."

Davida flushed and stammered. She'd always liked Sarah's father, but his manner of speech, usually faintly ironic, often left her not sure exactly what he meant. She had the strong impression he wasn't really surprised to see her, in spite of his words. Yet how could he possibly have known she was coming?

How on earth could she propose to this intimidating man? Suppose he had never been the least bit serious? Confused and suddenly shy, Davida couldn't decide where to look.

Lord Harwood laughed lightly at her discomposure. "Let me make things a little easier for you, Davie. Your father and a handsome young whelp named Pelham were here late last night, or I should say, earlier this morning."

Davida gulped. "They were?" She had not thought it possible that her father could guess her whereabouts, much less catch up with her so soon. And why was Pelham with him? She fought down the sense of hope that tried to invade her. She would permit herself no more of this failure to face reality.

"Yes, and I may add, frantic with worry over you. Your father looked ready to fall over, from having ridden so hard."

Stricken with remorse, Davida began to wring her hands. "Oh, Your Grace, I'm so sorry, and sorry I've awakened you so early, and, and . . ." Tears began to flow.

He placed an arm around her and hugged her, offering her his handkerchief at the same time. After giving her a few minutes to compose herself, he put her gently away, took the kerchief from her, and dried her eyes.

"Now, Davie. I am quite abominably curious. Just cut line and tell me why you are here."

"S-s-sorry to be such a watering pot, Your Grace." Davida straightened her shoulders, drew in a deep breath, and poured her heart out to Sarah's father.

He listened without comment or obvious emotion until she had completed her explanation.

"So you've decided you'll take me up on my offer rather than marry Pelham?"

"Yes, that is if it was a real offer. Or were you just teasing?" Anxious blue eyes searched his face.

Lord Harwood studied her gravely for a long moment. "It would be the marriage of May and—if not December, at least September. It's just too ridiculous, isn't it? You laughed when I said it, you know."

"I . . . I thought it was just a joke. It was Sarah put it in my mind you might be serious."

"And what was Sarah's opinion of her doddering old

papa marrying her best friend?" Lord Harwood drawled
the words, irony lacing his tone.

Davida winced. "I have been very stupid, Your Grace.
I am so embarrassed." Her attempt to leave was quickly
parried by Harwood's gentle but firm grasp of her shoulders as he pushed her back down onto the settee beside
him.

"There's no need for you to be embarrassed, Davida.
Rather, I should be. No man likes to think of being
ridiculed by his daughter."

"But she didn't, Your Grace. Not at all. She actually
seemed to like the idea of our always being close, and of
your not being left alone when she married. Though I
warned her I would be a wicked stepmother." Davida
wrinkled her face into a vicious grimace and then twinkled a smile up at the duke when he barked with laughter.

"Minx." He flicked her nose with his finger, then
abruptly grew serious. "Tell me, Davida, what sort of
marriage did you envision when you came here this
morning?"

"I'm not sure I take your meaning?"

He cleared his throat and gazed into the distance for a
moment, then turned to her. "Were you hoping for a marriage in name only, rather than for a more intimate connection, one that might result in children, for example."

"Would . . . would you want children, Your Grace?"
Davida inquired timidly, eyes lowered and a flush
spreading over her cheeks. "That is, Sarah thought you
were . . . ah, that you would want companionship."

A faint unreadable smile crossed his face and then
faded. "Well, of course, companionship is a very important part of a good marriage, but you are not answering
my question, Davida, my dear."

Thinking aloud, she mused, "It is not as if you *need*
children. You have often said your brother's three sons
more than satisfactorily secured the succession. But I,

well, I have always wanted children. But I don't have to have them, I suppose. Oh, I just don't know."

Davida grew agitated. "I really wasn't thinking very clearly about you, about us."

"No, you were thinking of your young man. You love him very much, don't you?"

"Yes." Davida lifted eyes filled with tears to him. "But as I said, I don't want to be married to him when he loves another. He might grow to hate me."

"Yet you offer me the same fate."

"Please forgive me, Your Grace. It was very wrong of me." Choked with tears, Davida tried once more to rise, and was once more gently restrained.

This time Harwood pulled her into his arms and tenderly stroked her hair as she wept. "No, no, you mustn't cry. You may be in the right, you know. Your young man might be miserable with you if he loves another. He seemed very concerned about you last night, but it could just be that he felt responsible."

Now it seemed as if it was the duke's turn to think out loud. "I can't imagine you giving me any grief. You have such a sweet, giving nature, you see. You would do your best to be a good wife to me, I know. I'm sure I could be very happy with you."

"Then . . . what are you saying, Your Grace?" Davida raised her head and looked into the eyes of a man she'd known all her life. There was tenderness and compassion there.

"I am saying that if you truly wish it, I would be very pleased to make you my wife."

"Oh! Thank you, Your Grace. I do wish it." Davida sat up, pulling away from him. "I shall do my best to see you never regret it."

"There is still a very important unresolved issue here, however." The Duke of Harwood's expression was determined.

Her blush clearly told him that Davida knew exactly

what he meant. "But I can't be the one to decide. I mean, if you aren't . . . that is if you can't . . . I mean, I would understand, and, as you say, companionship . . ."

Lord Harwood chuckled and cupped Davida's chin in one large hand, bending his face near hers. But what he might have said or done was interrupted by the butler's stentorian tones announcing, "Lord Pelham and Sir Charles Gresham."

Rushing into the room, Sir Charles burst out, "Davida, I don't know whether to hug you or to beat you." He pulled her into his arms and held her tight.

"My precious girl, racketing about England alone. Thank God you've come to no harm."

"Oh, Papa, I'm so sorry I worried you." A look at his haggard face and Davida was sunk in shame at her thoughtless action. "Is Mama . . . ?"

"She's in London, anxiously awaiting news. I've sent a messenger to tell her you've been found. But what can you have been about, child?" Sir Charles looked from her to the duke.

Pelham stood surveying this scene from the doorway. The relief that had flooded him when Harwood's messenger had arrived was beginning to be replaced by anger. Like Sir Charles he wanted to shake Davida and embrace her all at the same time. Denied the outlet of the embrace, his emotions erupted in anger. "Yes, what *can* you have been about? Your parents and I have been in agony over your disappearance. Such selfish behavior is inexcusable. And what did you mean in your note about a 'more favorable match'?"

Harwood reached past Sir Charles to take Davida's hand and pull her to his side. "Davida has done me the honor of consenting to be my wife." The characteristic ironic twist he gave to "consenting" caused Davida to look up into his face questioningly.

"Indeed you two walked in before I could claim my engagement kiss." He lowered his head and tipped a very surprised Davida's face up so he could press a brief, firm kiss on her lips.

"You come in good time, Lord Pelham, and Sir Charles, old friend, to wish us happy."

Chapter Twenty-two

"Oh, no you don't." Pelham was almost purple with fury as he bounded across the room. "Davida is promised to me."

Sir Charles quickly moved between the two men. "Please, Lord Pelham. Control yourself. No call for violence."

"None at all," the duke drawled urbanely. "Let us all sit and discuss this in a civilized manner." Harwood did not look the least discomposed by Pelham's outburst.

"I think we will all be much more able to deal intelligently with matters after we have broken our fast." He gestured for the others to seat themselves while he rang for breakfast.

Thoughts in turmoil, Davida had the oddest fancy as they sat stiffly waiting until they could be served and be private again. She thought that they were like one of those quartets in the opera, each member singing of his or her own emotions. The idea of the four of them suddenly bursting into song amused her and somehow had a calming effect on her. She dared a glance at Pelham, who was still glaring furiously at the duke.

What would he sing of, she wondered. Why had he come? Why was he still insisting on their engagement? No one would possibly blame him for crying off after her unchaperoned flight. She felt a faint flicker of hope, which she once again sternly repressed, being determined to face facts.

Pelham's thoughts were very uncomfortable. *The man is too old for Davida, can't she see that? A distinguished-looking man, though.* Somehow he made Pelham feel like a callow youth. He glanced at Sir Charles and was alarmed but not surprised that Davida's father was looking quite pleased, his gaze moving from Davida to the duke and back again.

Damn all. The man had spent a good deal of the time on their harrowing ride in pursuit of Davida lamenting his unfortunate obsession with a title for her. "Many a fine young buck would have courted her, but no, I had to run them off. Only a title or a fortune or both would do for *my* girl. She don't care. She's always wanted to please me, but not at all ambitious for herself." There had been a great deal more in this vein.

Sir Charles had sworn that if he got his daughter back safe and sound he'd let her choose her own husband and never raise a single objection.

Now his eyes were wide, his expression was bemused, and Pelham could just hear him thinking, *My daughter, Duchess of Harwood.*

Pelham turned toward Davida. She had a lost, confused look on her face. She looked tiny and young and terribly innocent next to the tall, sophisticated Duke of Harwood. Pelham felt something move fiercely through his whole being. *I love her,* he realized. *I can't bear to let any other man have her, and especially an old man she doesn't love!* Hands clenched, he began to think frantically. How was he to prevent losing the woman he loved to this handsome, urbane, and outstandingly eligible duke?

After their tray was carried in, Davida, hands shaking a little, poured tea and coffee, and the four helped themselves to sweet biscuits and croissants.

"Now then," drawled the duke after these formalities were completed, "as I see it, the problem is that Davida has one too many fiancés. Yet she gave me to understand that she had terminated her engagement to you, Lord Pelham."

"She has a mistaken notion that I want to marry another woman. I don't! I want to marry her." He spoke calmly now, but with conviction.

"Oh, Monty, stop." Davida held out her hands in a supplicating gesture. "Don't you see, now you can marry Elspeth. You love her, I know you do. Papa wouldn't let me cry off before, but now he will, won't you, Papa."

Sir Charles looked somewhat embarrassed. "Never meant to force you to wed Pelham, my girl. Just thought it would work out. The boy seems genuinely fond of you, you know."

"He's fond of me, and I . . . am fond of him, too. We can be friends, can't we, Monty?" She looked at him appealingly.

Before Pelham could find the exact words to convince Davida that it was her love, not her friendship he wanted, her father broke in. "Sly puss. Never let me know Harwood had offered for you," he chuckled.

"I thought he was just teasing. I'm still not sure he wasn't then, but he's being very kind to . . ."

"Kind!" Pelham exploded. "He'd be deucedly lucky to have you for a wife and he knows it." He jumped from his chair and strode toward Davida. "But I won't let you marry this old lecher, Davida. You promised to marry me, and I mean to hold you to it."

"Old lecher! Oh, Monty, how unfair." She stood facing him defiantly, small fists clenched. "His Grace is not in the least like that. In fact, he wants a companion, someone to keep him from being alone when Sarah marries." She tossed her head and glared at her erstwhile fiancé.

Pelham made a derisive noise. "And pigs can fly," he snarled.

Harwood interrupted. "Children, children. No shouting, please. Charles, I think if we left these two alone for a few minutes they might be able to sort things out."

"What? Oh, yes." Sir Charles rose somewhat reluctantly.

"But before I go, Davida, it is only fair to clear up one important point. May we be private a moment?" He glanced at the other two, not really waiting for permission, and then took Davida's elbow and led her across the room, to stand by the large bow window that looked out over the rose garden.

"Thank you for defending me from the charge of lechery," he began, the curve of his mouth and his tone lacing his words with their usual irony. "I agree that Lord Pelham does not do me justice in giving me that name. But you may be expecting, and in fact hoping for, a very convenient sort of marriage, a marriage in name only, in fact. Is that true?"

Not knowing how to answer him, Davida stood with her head bowed, listening, feeling her cheeks grow progressively pinker with each word.

"I know, Davie, that I seem old to you. But I am only thirty-nine, by no means in my dotage. I am able to be a husband to you in every way, and so I mean to be, if you decide to have me. Do you understand what I am saying?"

Deeply embarrassed, as much by her näiveté as by the import of the duke's words, Davida could only nod mutely, wide blue eyes barely meeting Harwood's before she lowered them to study the pattern in the thick Aubusson carpet at her feet. Surely she had never blushed as she blushed now.

"Well, then, you must listen carefully to what your young man has to say. If you would accept a bit of friendly advice?"

"Yes, of course."

"It may very well be that Lord Pelham is deeply attracted to Lady Elspeth but rationally knows she is the wrong sort of wife for him. If that be the case, and he freely chooses to marry you, it is unlikely that he would resent you or hate you, as you seem to fear."

"Do you think not?" Hope flickered again in her heart.

"No, I don't. Nor do I think he merely intends to marry you out of a misguided sense of honor. I get the strong impression he cares for you. But if you still feel uncomfortable with the idea of marrying him after this interview, I will be honored to make you my wife."

He kissed her hands one after the other, bowed low, and strolled over to Sir Charles. "Come, old friend. I have a magnificent new stallion to show you. Arabian blood, fine lineage."

Alone in the drawing room, Davida and Pelham let the silence settle around them. The soft crunch of his boots on the fine carpet warned Davida that he was approaching her at the window, where she stood staring out at the formal garden, not really seeing it.

"Davie?"

She turned and lifted troubled eyes to meet his.

"Davie, you can't marry that old lecher."

"He isn't old and he isn't a lecher."

"It is clear enough he desires you. I have eyes, Davida."

"And it is clear enough that Elspeth desires you and you desire her. Why are you here? Why aren't you with her now, planning your wedding?"

"Because I don't want to marry her. How many times do I have to tell you that?"

"In the Raleighs' gardens, I saw you take her into your arms and kiss her."

"You saw her pull me off balance so that I had to grasp her to keep from falling. And it was she who kissed me."

"Do give over, Monty." Davida stamped her foot with frustration. "I heard what you said to one another, too."

"What you heard was what Elspeth wanted you to hear."

"I know, but that doesn't mean it wasn't true. You did say it would be shabby not to marry me now, didn't you, Monty? And you did kiss her on the very day you told me you didn't love her anymore, the very day you kissed me in—oh! such a way—that evening in the Malcolms' garden." Davida's cheeks burned with remembered desire and present embarrassment.

"It's true, all of it. But it isn't what you think. Hear me out, please! She threw herself at me that afternoon. She came to my home, veiled, and lay in wait for me. I did kiss her, but it was really that kiss that set the seal on the end of our relationship. I was even more sure then that it was you I wanted. And what little feeling I had for her, you may be sure she killed forever with that perfidious performance in the Raleighs' garden."

"How can I believe you? I didn't hear you contradict her when she said that you loved her, but felt honor-bound to marry me."

"I was taken unawares. She spoke to me quite calmly, held her hand out and said she wanted to be friends. When she asked for a last kiss, all I could think of was how to get rid of her. She saw you coming up behind me and made sure what you saw and heard confirmed your fears."

"Lord Pelham." Davida drew herself up and looked at him sternly. "There is no more need to continue this charade. I have a much better offer now. You no longer have any responsibility to marry me. In fact . . ." She tensed and cleared her throat. "In fact, you'd be doing me a favor to release me."

"No! You don't mean that! I won't believe that of you." Pelham grabbed her and pulled her into his arms. "Davida, I realized something a few minutes ago. Hold still, look at me."

She was struggling in his arms, turning her head away

from his mesmerizing eyes, his tempting lips. She wouldn't let desire master her, not this time.

Emotion charged Pelham's voice as he sought to convince her. "I haven't lied to you, not once. I made up my mind not to marry Elspeth after the picnic. My proposal was precipitated by her engagement announcement, I admit, but I'd already decided to commence courting you."

"Pooh! When was this resolution taken?" Davida leaned back as far away from him as he would allow her, blue eyes flashing.

"The night before, when I learned you'd turned Curzon down. But that's not important now. That decision was entirely a practical one. You seemed a good sort of girl. I thought we'd suit. My feelings weren't engaged."

"Not by me, at any rate."

He gave her a slight shake. "Not by any one. But now . . . a few minutes ago, when I saw how pleased your father was at the duke's announcement, I realized I might lose you. That's when I suddenly knew. Oh, Davie, please believe me, darling. I love you. Sometime in these last few weeks I've gone from feeling you were an excellent choice for a wife, to feeling I can't live without you. Do you hear me? I love you!"

"No, you don't," Davida gasped, her eyes meeting and being held by his cobalt gaze. "You're just saying it because you feel honorbound to marry me."

"I love you with all my heart. I don't want anyone else, and I won't let anyone else have you. Look, I'll prove it." He bent his head and kissed her, a gentle but searing kiss that went straight to her heart. Feeling her näive but eager response, he whispered against her lips, "And I think you love me, too."

"Oh, Monty, that's not fair."

He drew his head back, still holding her snugly in his arms. "Why not, my love?"

"Because I can't think straight when you kiss me like that."

In response, he kissed her again, more insistently, his lips moving restlessly, demandingly over hers.

Davida felt her knees go weak. It seemed her bones were turning to liquid. She swayed against Pelham and opened her lips to his teasing tongue. With gentle expertise he stroked and tantalized her until she felt that she had been set afire.

Pelham broke off with a groan. They were both breathing heavily. "Your fudsy old duke can't make you feel like this, Davida. And Elspeth never could make me feel the way I do when I kiss you."

"That . . . that's not love, though, is it? It's lust. Oh, please don't." Davida moaned, trying to pull away. He held her close, dropping kisses along her cheek, down her jawline, along her slender neck. Unable to resist him any longer, Davida turned her head to give him access to her lips, pressing against him wantonly.

"I love you, Davie. I love you and I want you, and in three days' time I'm going to have you."

She groaned softly and lifted her face for another kiss. "Ah, yes, Monty. Yes!"

For a long time they stood thus, letting their love for each other take them to dizzying heights of excitement. At last Pelham had to call a halt. "Sweetheart, we've got to stop, or we'll scandalize the elegant Duke of Harwood by consummating our marriage right here on his carpet."

A little unsteadily, Davida stepped back and looked at her beloved's face. His eyes were almost black with desire. She shook her head to clear it and walked away a few steps. Then suddenly she thought, *I've let him do it again, I've let him get around me with kisses.* She turned back and launched herself at him, pummeling him angrily.

"You! You are the lecher. Kissing me, then Elspeth, then me! You had better not still be wearing the willow for her after kissing me like that! You know I love you, so you think you can get around me by seducing me!"

He dodged her blows, laughing, as he tried to catch her hands. "Only you, sweetheart. I want only you, love only you."

"That had better be the truth, after all the trouble I've gone to, jilting you and proposing to a duke, no less, so you could have a free choice. You'd better choose me because you really want me instead of her, or I'll . . . I'll . . ." She jerked free and flailed at him again.

"You'll beat me to a bloody pulp, it seems. And I would deserve it." He captured her hands and twisted them behind her. "Have you been taking lessons from Gentleman Jackson, my jealous little termagant?"

"I will if I need to. I'm not going to be a complacent wife, Monty. If you marry me, don't expect to chase after Elspeth or any other woman."

"I wouldn't dare." His face was bright with amusement and admiration."

"No fancy pieces!"

"No."

"No muslin company."

"No, no, no." He kissed her again. "I won't want anyone but you." He released her hands, and they crept up to curve around his neck.

She relaxed and leaned against him, looking up at him adoringly. "Truly?"

"Truly! Word of honor. I love you, Davie."

"Oh, Monty, I love you so. I was miserable when I thought I had to give you up."

"Hmmm. It begins to look as if I've lost a fiancée."

The two lovers turned to see the Duke of Harwood and Sir Charles standing in the doorway.

Pelham put a protective arm about Davida. "You may wish us happy, Your Grace." There was a certain wariness in his look as he faced the older man.

"Indeed, I do wish you happy." Sternly, Harwood continued, "If you can't be happy with the love of a good-natured, affectionate girl like Davida, you are a young fool."

"I assure you, Your Grace, I am no fool."

"No, you don't look to be one, unfortunately for me. Well, then, congratulations. Davida, I take it you are satisfied with your choice of bridegrooms?"

Davida looked worriedly at the duke. She had never been able to guess his true feelings. Had she hurt him or was he relieved to be free of the necessity of marrying her?

"Yes, Your Grace. I am very satisfied, but I am sorry . . . that is, I'm afraid I put you to a great deal of bother."

"Do not refine too much upon it." He took her hand, and she thought she saw a flash of regret in his eyes before he schooled himself. He bowed over her hand but did not touch her fingertips. Then he stepped back, a crooked smile on his face.

"Actually, Davie, you've done me a great favor. You've jarred me out of my self-imposed isolation. Since Eleanor died five years ago, I've not let myself think of marrying again, but now you've put me in the mood for it, I think I'll go to London next season and look over the field."

Davida smiled her approval. "I'm sure Sarah will be happy to hear that, Your Grace."

Slowly, almost fearfully, the young couple turned to her father. "Papa?" Davida took a step toward him.

He drew her into his arms for a vigorous hug. "Are you sure this is what you want?"

"Yes, Papa. You aren't disappointed I won't be a duchess, are you?"

"I've been a foolish old man, Davida. Just be happy and I'll be content."

Pelham pulled his fiancée back against his side, a possessive hand at her waist. "It will be my privilege to make Davida happy, sir." He murmured for her ear alone, "And my pleasure."

Pink-cheeked, Davida smiled up at him. Then, boldly, she turned so she could whisper in his ear, "Mine, too!"

Epilogue

"What did the post bring, dearest?" Lord Pelham slipped up behind his wife and nuzzled her neck, his arms wrapped around her waist.

"I put your mail on your desk. I have a letter from Sarah to both of us."

"How is she?"

"Well, I suppose. I was surprised to learn she is in London for the season. She and Gregory Allensby have apparently quarreled. She's seeing that handsome equerry, Lord Meade. And her father is pursuing Lady Cornwall, who swore she'd never marry again."

"Indeed, that does sound fascinating."

"She wants to know when we are coming to town. she says it is sadly flat without us, with all in mourning for Princess Charlotte."

"Perhaps we shouldn't this season. What about our little pledge of affection?" He allowed his hand to stray past her waist, curving over the slightly rounded contours of her body. "The future Baron Pelham must be born at Pelham Manor, you know."

"Only for a month? We have plenty of time, really."

"Hmmm. Perhaps for a month or so, if it would please you. There are some matters coming before the House of Lords that I'd like to have a say in."

Davida smiled and turned her head to kiss him on the cheek. In a hesitant voice she announced, "She . . . she mentions Lady Elspeth."

"What of her?" Pelham's voice was sharp with annoyance. He thought his wife still believed he had feelings for Elspeth, and it was so far from the truth as to be a source of aggravation.

"She wed Lord Whitham privately a week ago."

"Poor Whit."

"Monty!" Davida laughed over her shoulder at him.

"I mean it, Davie. He's a poor sot. It seems to me that after we've been blissfully married for almost a year, you wouldn't still get that shadowed, sad look on your face whenever Elspeth is mentioned." His aggrieved tone and unhappy look touched her deeply.

She turned into his arms, hushing him with a kiss. No longer the kiss of a naïve girl, it soon had them both breathless. She pulled back first and caressed the slight cleft in his chin lovingly with her forefinger as she whispered, "I do believe you. Truly, Monty, I do. But I so hope she'll be happy. You see, I feel guilty because I have you, and she doesn't."

"Is *that* why you always look so uncomfortable when she is under discussion?"

She smiled and leaned against him, nodding her head. "I'm always so glad that Elspeth jilted you, you see."

"And I am always so glad I was jilted." The hunger in his deep cobalt gaze had the power to make her pulse race. A little embarrassed by the turn her thoughts were taking, she moved away from him, lifting the letter to continue reading from it.

"And I'm glad you jilted me, too."

That brought her up short. "You are?" Davida wrinkled her nose in puzzlement.

"Yes, for if you hadn't run off like that, there is no telling how long it would have taken for me to realize how much I love you, or how much longer after *that* it would have taken to convince you of the fact. I believe our marriage got off to a much better start because of your escapade, dangerous though it was."

She smiled. "I'd never thought of it that way, but I believe you are right."

"And now you are trying to jilt me again."

"Wh . . . what?"

"Come, now, little wife. You've been married long enough to know that that kiss, ah, raised certain expectations, and yet you are trying to drift off with that letter as if you plan to answer it forthwith."

She fluttered her eyelashes for an instant, coquettishly. "I can't think what you are hinting at, my lord."

Pelham's strong hands closed around her upper arms, and he drew her to him. "Look at me, Lady Pelham," he commanded.

When she raised now-serious sunlit blue eyes to him, he demanded, "Come upstairs with me, Davida."

"At this time of day?" Davida's tone pretended astonishment, but she nestled into her husband's embrace and received his ardent kiss. Then she whispered something in his ear which made him smile, and they walked up the stairs arm in arm.